THE CHOSEN CHILD: TALES OF OCAIA

K.J. Riley

Ocaia Publishing

Copyright © 2020 K.J. Riley

All rights reserved

The characters and events portrayed in this book are fictitious. Any similarity to real persons, living or dead, is coincidental and not intended by the author.

No part of this book may be reproduced, or stored in a retrieval system, or transmitted in any form or by any means, electronic, mechanical, photocopying, recording, or otherwise, without express written permission of the publisher.

ISBN: 9798555645722
Imprint: Independently published

Cover design by: Shoham David "Leo" Charikar
Library of Congress Control Number: 2018675309
Printed in the United States of America

Dedicated to my children.

May you chase your dreams and choose the path best suited for you. Always know that we love you, forever and always.

Prologue

Takenna slumbered in eternal darkness, knowing not where she was in space and time. Her dreams became nightmares - death, despair, and war. No matter how she tried to stir herself awake, the misery continued and increased with ferocity. One by one, she witnessed the fall of humankind. One by one, she watched the loss of plant and animal life. Innocence vanished as quickly as it began, and each life snuffed out tugged at her heart.

There it was in the distance, a light off the horizon growing in size and color intensity. Bright white shot through clouds and increased in hues of yellow, orange, and blood red. It was coming closer. She tried to shield herself, but stiffness of her sleep prevented such movement. She was frozen, unable to run or hide. As the light and heat came sweltering toward her, despair for her own life swelled inside. As she was unable to save lives of those she watched, she too was unable to save herself. Just as the wave of light came to envelope her being, a thunderous noise erupted around her darkness. Her eyes opened and her body ached. Gasping for breath and searching around her, terrified of the light that came and went so abruptly, it was gone.

Takenna fell to her knees and wept, her translucent blue hair covered her face as she shook her head from left to right. For all that she had witnessed and the feeling that this would be her inevitable end as well, the anguish of those raw emotions poured out of her all at once. She held herself tight, weeping in anxiousness and sorrow while in her mind the nightmares played

over and over again. After what seemed an eon, she released the tight grasp of herself and slowly began to scan her current environment. Clear and ongoing hues of rainbow light as far as the eye could see. The air was pure, the picturesque glow in soft light began to sooth the soul, and Takenna was able to regain her composure. She stood, struggling it seemed with the weight of images still in her mind, consciously attempting to regain all of her strength. All at once, she knew what she had to do. Her time had come.

For the fourth time, the planet had a clean slate. Takenna's brothers before her had attempted, and failed, to maintain a sustainable existence within the confines of this planetary realm. Staring at the rock in space, contemplating how all attempts at life and beginning had come to a dramatic end each time. What lessons learned can be counteracted and improved upon? Conflict seemed inevitable. This was a formula she accounted for in the calculation of her canvas. There is never true peace within the hearts of those that dwell amongst each other, a burden learned in all of the trials made here time and time again.

A voice rang loud and clear, echoing throughout the crystal void. "Takenna," it said, "how will you proceed?"

She closed her eyes, gentle and slow as she centered her soul, her lashes interlacing as a calmness flowed through her entire being. A reimagining of this land was in her total control. A desire to create utopia, knowing it would never truly be as such but giving her best attempt, she wanted her children to feel as passionate as she did in this moment of awakening. Determination and vigor from within, she threw her arms into the air and spoke her truth. As soft as she appeared, her voice became as intense and thunderous as the one that preceded her own.

As I am one, so shall be the land, air, and sea.
As I am at peace, so shall the dwellers be.
As I am their storm, so shall it bring them serenity.
As I Takenna, their mother, so shall be for all eternity.

She struck her hands together above her head, the clashing sound created a spiraling wind around her and straight to the planet ahead. The land began to move together and puzzle-piece itself into one contiguous place. Water swayed and crashed into places it had not been in quite some time. Tufts of white and grey swirled around in the calamity, creating a creamy picture high above the morphing of the land below. After a few moments, the dance of elements below had come to a halt and her first step had been completed. Takenna straightened her posture and stood proud in admiration of her work. After a thoughtful pause, she was ready to begin the next phase of her process. Creation of life.

Takenna closed her eyes once more and then opened them to find herself walking the lands of her new planet. This blank slate would hold a few good things that her brothers before her had produced, but most of it would be new to her children. A mixture of old and new beings, molded and created to be able to bring diversity into balance. Though the nightmares weighed heavily on her heart, she remembered some good things. Humans had vivid imaginations and were able to transcribe words and pictures to be able to tell their stories. Some of those stories, although not created by a Creator, were rather charming and she wanted to implement some of those aspects as well.

With every step she took a shade of green sprang beneath her. The harder her weight pressed into the ground, the darker the green would appear to become. Her smile created new flowers on the ground, and when she giggled at the same time those flowers tended to have a gentle glow on the petals. Each flower varied in size and color, from the palest of pink to the darkest shade of purple. Her favorite was the glimmering blue flower with short petals and a long stem, the scent of which she felt echoed the essence of her being. Takenna looked to the sky and gently blew out air between her lips, a soft breeze that graced the air and tingled her senses. The intersections of land that came together had done a marvelous job of molding large rock formations, but with a raise of her hand she made them grow taller and more bold. Large and small trees were created between her hands, lifting the dirt and growing them taller, and her laughter brought the tops of them to life in color and movement. Trees in her likeness were more colorful than her predecessors, hues that resembled the place of her waking to remind her children just how beautiful life can be. Each small tear of joy shed during her experience created a variation of pools, rivers, and tiny ponds over the land.

Satisfied with the landscape, she then focused on the life of creatures to wander within the world. She had seen three previous sets of lives and wanted hers to be superior in all aspects. She stilled her breath, closed her eyes once more, and raised her hands and let the emotions flow out of her soul. Wind whirled around her silken hair, light flitted through the trees and shimmering dust emerged from her fingertips to be carried throughout the world. The sea rumbled against the land she had formed with the new disturbance in the air. With seamless binding, particles of dust clumped together in various areas of land and sea to create what Takenna felt in her heart to be the purest forms of life. The moments ticked by as she poured every piece of her heart and soul into her final creations and standing tall in the blustering air around her.

Stillness fell over her and the air retreated, slowly grazing between the leaves of trees and through the mountains. Eyes still shut, there was no need to see them now as she had an eternity to watch over her children. With a deep inhale and pause, she opened her eyes back to crystal void from whence she began.

She called this place Ocaia.

Prima Dair

   Long blades of grass in variant shades in green and yellow swayed in the graceful breeze. Pockets of treed areas fell sparse across the land, easily spotted due to the sheer size and color rising above the land. Trees of pink to the West and purple to the East, a marker for the tribe of Prima Dair, the Dolgaian, to know their general direction when exploring their territory. Flowers dotted across the land in vibrant colors, a scenic landscape for those that dwell across the expansive land. Birds crossed the plains above the grass and through the air.
  Large, deep green birds with sprawling tail feathers and spiked head feathers kept a wide berth from the Dolgaian and were wary of other animals. These were mostly ground dwellers, pecking in the ground to find their food. However, the could fly if they desired and could sometimes be seen perched among the tree branches above.
  Similar in size and shape, flocks like the evening sky in color glistened among the treetops, with feathers that changed in the light from oranges, pinks and reds and wisps springing from the back of their crown. These flying birds were elusive, staying among the trees until dusk and then flying in the fading light.
  Smaller birds flew in sporadic movement with no clear direction, shorter in length with beaks that were almost as long as their entire body, wings moving so quickly they almost appeared to be colorless. They flew among the grasslands and kissed the pep-

pulas for a quick drink before making flight elsewhere. These birds nested in lower tree branches, but were so small that they were barely visible upon first glance.

Medium sized birds resided among the trees as well, larger wings with sharp angles and twin tail feathers to cut through the air with ease, and short-pointed beaks meant for eating insects. Sweet sounds of chirping came from their beaks as they glided across the plains, delighted to dwell in the open land below them. Colors of vibrant greens, yellows, and pinks swooped across the lands as they sang their songs.

The largest birds had giant wings with a large spanning bone and a hook on the top with vein-like lines from the top to the bottom edges. They did not bear feathers like their flying kinship but were sleek and flat against their skin in various colors and shades. Their four feet were large to carry the great weight of these beasts as they walked across the land, long talons sprawling out to grasp the land and trees large enough to hold their size. Their heads were massive with pronounced teeth exposed through their mouth, and grass-like spines flowed down their backs to the tip of their giant and bulky tail. Trees grew from the top of the crown outward and upward toward the sky, cascading delicate beauty over their piercing eyes, and no two birds looked alike. These birds did not travel too close to the center of Prima Dair and made their home further North, nesting within the trees to the Eastern rim.

The Dolgaian were a tribe of simple farmers and

foragers, utilizing the soil to make their living. Unlike the other tribes on Ocaia, they had fingers on their paws which allowed them to create tools and gather crops. Large ears graced the top of their slender faces and allowed for heightened sense of danger. Their snout protruded forward with a black nose and modest mouth. Eyes large and round were shades of dark to light brown. Reddish-brown tints of color covered their underbelly fur and raised to the tips in shades of green and yellow to serve as camouflage to their environment. Powerful hind legs with large hooves allowed great speed whether upright or on all fours. Their tail, too, sporting the greens and yellows through the bushiness that mimicked the sway of the tall grasslands.

Prima Dair had an optimal position in Ocaia. The lands were open enough to create farming lands, and lush with fruit to supply additional food source. Josima Mora to the North was much colder and the terrain treacherous with powder. The Savidi Mor was to the East, separating the land from the large mountains on the other side and leading to the Eye of Takenna, the holy site of the Goddess of Life. To the West were the Tuskula Mountains, which were smaller in size and led to the Pati Maio waters. Joto was neighboring to the South, seemingly close but far enough away that the tribes did not cross paths unless bartering with each other at market, overgrown with tall trees of orange and red leaves. Takii was far North and East, bearing lands of variant grasslands and trees. Axel Hoxa was also far East, lands of dirt and sparse grasses lie there and bordered the great waters of Pati Tailo.

When palawals came of age, assimilation into the tribe and taking on a career were key to the survival of the Dolgaian. It was an honor to all to become one with the tribe and work toward building their own gean, a family. There were, however, some that contest this tradition and believe there is no place of assimilation for them within the tribe.

❖ ❖ ❖

Large ears took in the sounds of birds bustling through the land. Large eyes closed, focused on other senses taking in the light without sight. Scion's tail flipped up and down in tandem with the grass blades. Laying on his belly, he soaked up the oreon light on his yellow backside in a trance with the happenings around him. He opened his eyes, sparkling in the lightest shade of gold, watching a lanarai bug dance in front of his black nose.

Sweet air blew across the green covered land and filled Scion with a sense of bliss. His nose sucked in the wind as it wafted by, catching the lanarai in his breath, and then he exhaled with a smile across his face. The breeze tickled his ears and, with the faint and succulent smell of honey tarfe, made his stomach rumble. Looking up to the oreon, it was well passed time to eat. Picking up his tarp and tack, he began the trek back to Prima Dair.

His trot was bouncy with joy, skipping and spinning his way through the tall-bladed grass. Flittering through the air and dancing on the breeze were butterflies of bright green with black on the tips of their wings. Flying to and fro, flapping their large wings and shining in the oreon, and landing on peppulas for a drink. The top wings were arched with a graceful curve and the bottom wings had a large teardrop on the end. Scion watched them flutter by as he crossed the open grassland. A pinkish-yellow bird darter right in front of Scion and gave him pause as he watched the bird tear through the air and up into a nearby tree. He looked upon the bird with such admiration of its freedom.

Hopping across the rocks at Mizon Creek and dancing through the blush peppulas, Scion decided to pluck up a bouquet for Caipri. He could just imagine her swooning over the quaint gift and then swiftly pushing him away when realizing he was making her fall in love with him. The thought alone gave him a chuckle as he pictured her face trying to hide behind her stature. She was a tough one to crack, but none fairer and sweeter resided in their land in his mind. He was determined to make his first love a part of his new gean.

After a brisk walk through the grasslands, he entered his homeland. Scion walked purposefully through the Prima Dair Kaian to find Caipri. Her usual pass through at this time of day was by the Fountain of Takenna. She was devout to the Goddess of Life and sang her prayers daily. As expected, Caipri was there and in the middle of her evening song. He watched and waited patiently, holding the bouquet behind his back. As Caipri raised her head to finish her nightly song, Scion approached. He gently gave the Goddess of Life his praise as well and then turned his attention to his love.

"Takenna guides you, Sesuna." He took her paw, touched his forehead to her knuckle, and then released her. "I saw these peppulas on my way back from Mizon Creek today. They are not as beautiful as the Sesuna, but they made me think of you."

Scion presented the bouquet to Caipri. She stood and paused, paw fingers clutched together in front of her body, tension in her stance as she looked at him and then the peppulas. He could see the different scenarios running through her mind as he held them out to her. She took a step forward, retrieved the bouquet, but no smile graced her face. She raised the peppulas to her nose, took in a deep breath, and then gazed at Scion over the tops of the lush petals.

"Scion," she said, "how many times must I tell you that these charming tactics are really unnecessary?"

"As many times as I give you charm, my sweet." Scion winked as he bowed in her direction, his bow went low in a show of exceeding effort and slightly amusing mockery.

"Well, my pet, I accept your generous peppulas, but you really must cease these acts of kindness on my behalf. Are there not others more deserving of such an act?"

Scion stood from his bow, as tall as he could muster,

raising a paw across his chest and the other behind his haunches. "Perhaps there are others of great deserving. However, my eyes see only one." He slapped down the paw from across his chest and then turned on his hooves to head to his dorsa, quickly in an effort to keep Caipri from a snappy retort. A sly smirk crossed his mouth as he paced through the Kaian and back to his dorsa. Scion was confident that he would wear her down, eventually.

He entered through the door and hung his tarp and tack. The smell of Jiana's honey tarfe filled the air within and Scion suddenly realized how famished he was from his day of exploration. He quickly bumped off the dirt from his hooves before walking to the table located in the middle of the room.

Jiana stood at the opposite end of the dorsa at the cutting table, making tarfe for dinner to provide for their gean. She was much like Scion, but taller and heftier. Jiana was the tallest female of the tribe, eyes of light gold color like his, and a scar across the back of her right ear, a reminder of how careless her brother could be. Her movement never ceased as she heard him enter the dorsa.

"So, Scion. What mischief did you get up to today?"

Jiana's tone had a not-so-unfamiliar ring to his ears. The inquiry itself led a little brother to antagonize his righteous sister. Scion took some tarfe off the table, bit into it and replied with his mouth full of food.

"Well, Jia, since you asked, I went to Mizon Creek for stroll. Beautiful day, if you ask me. Too bad you missed it while being cooped up here all through the oreon light."

Annoyed with his manners, but also knowing a reaction would prove futile when dealing with him, Jiana continued to make tarfe and never looked at him.

"A stroll? Meaningless and unproductive as always, Scion. With the amount of time spent fawning over our Sesuna, you could actually be assimilating with the Dolgaian and contribute to the tribe like everyone else."

Scion sat in a chair and propped his hooves onto the table, continuing to eat tarfe. He rather enjoyed Jiana's annoyance with him, but he enjoyed his freedom more.

"I could, but then I wouldn't be me and I'd be more like you," he stated while pointing tarfe behind his sister's head. "Wound up tight and unhappy with my Takenna Life. Sounds so... drab."

As Scion continued to eat, Jiana stopped her tarfe making, took in a deep inhale and then exhaled slowly to gather her emotions. Scion was no longer a palawal and needed to focus on his gean, both present and future. Long had she protected him, but no more. She turned to face him, but her head was down and her eyes shut as she addressed him.

"Scion," she said in nearly a whisper, "I love you. Midawal loves you. With Padiwal gone we need you. I cannot make enough tarfe to eat and barter to keep our gean going forever. Assimilation to the tribe will allow you to find your place within Prima Dair." Jiana opened her eyes and looked at Scion with intensity and peering into Scion's soul. "You cannot hold on to this fantasy that you will be with her. The Sesuna does not belong with our kind and must attend to her duties at the request of Takenna. That is how it has been and shall always be."

Scion had a mischievous smirk roll across his mouth when she concluded her small monologue. He finished his tarfe and said nothing. When done, he stood and then bowed at Jiana before returning to his cotoom.

Jiana and Scion's midawal held tightly to the wall as she rounded the corner. Shawartia had long passed her prime and struggled to walk and see clearly. Old age was noticeable by the hunch of her shoulders, shakiness of her hands, and squinting when looking about. Not to mention the white fur sprouting about her body. Shawartia's mind, however, was still as sharp as the dawn she became a member of the tribe. Hearing Jiana hard at work to feed their gean gave her peace and pride. She gazed around the dorsa, attempting to focus on objects in the low-lit environment, searching for Scion. It was traditional for all in the gean to dine together, and yet he was frequently absent.

"Scion will not be joining, then?"

"No, Midawal," Jiana replied.

Shawartia made her way to the table and sat down. "You act as though the fault is not your own. I heard some commotion earlier when he arrived."

Jiana was fed up with Scion and felt scorned from Midawal. She slammed her cutting blade down on the table and turned to Shawartia.

"Midawal! He gallivants his time away, dreaming to be with our Sesuna and refusing to assimilate. He is cowardly to refute his responsibility to the tribe and leave us holding the tarp empty. I cannot make enough tarfe for all. Why can he not see Takenna's light?"

"Takenna speaks to you of Scion, does she?" Curious amusement was wrapped in her tone with the inquiry to her palawal.

The question halted Jiana's emotions instantly. Why does that matter? With Midawal waiting for a response, she unclenched her fists and bowed her head.

"No, Midawal. She does not."

"Then, my beautiful palawal, we do not yet know Scion's place in Takenna's Life. She guides us all. He may not have the same path that we walk. Come. We eat and share with me the chatter of the Prima Dair Kaian. I am eager to hear the new gossip among the Dolgaian."

'Something'

Being a Sesuna or Sesuni was a rare gift and Caipri knew this. Born differently in shades of blue was a sign of being chosen by the Goddess of Life, Takenna. While her community bore the colors of their land in dark browns and bright greens, Caipri stood out like a thorn of the forest peppulas. Her colors were deep purple to cascading shades of iridescent blue at the tip of her fur. Her eyes were the piercing blue described like the ice within the nation of their Northern neighbors in Josima Mora. A Chosen Palawal of Takenna. She knew the duty she held to travel to the Eye of Takenna and a life of servitude to their Goddess. She had embraced this gift since she was a palawal, and yet her heart began to tug at a notion that she no longer wanted this life sentence.

Olicai was laying next to Caipri's resting bunk when she entered her cotoom, stirring her friend from a deep slumber. He raised his head, cocked it to the side as he watched her cross to the window, and then laid his back down. Olicai was found as a hatchling in the fields, alone and abandoned with his bright white fluff and blue-colored face. A few members had seen him and thought it was a sign for the Sesuna. Caipri was also very young when Olicai was gifted to her, and she nursed the hatching as he grew. Olicai looked much like the dark green birds that did not appear to fly, at least in the general shape of his body since his color was a stark contrast resembling the nima light with faint tints of purple and blue sheen on his feathers and a dark blue face now that he had matured. He was Caipri's companion and much smaller in size than the other wild birds of Prima Dair, making him perfect for walking or perching on her shoulders. The two had been practically inseparable since he was gifted to her, that is, except for when Olicai wanted to rest for long periods of time.

Caipri gazed out of her cotoom window at the Fountain of Takenna. The fountain was made from Ocaia ground, hardened and molded in a large circle. In the center, a model of Takenna, their Goddess of Life. Her hair elegantly designed in a much thinner mold to give the sense of fluidity as described in the ancient writings, and her hands gracefully arched above her head. Her body was shaped in Ocaia formations of trees, mountains, flowing waters and beautifully placed peppulas as their world was made in her likeness. Conflict within her grew as she waited for a sign from her Goddess to gain a sense of clarity, staring at the Fountain Goddess as if she would come to life and speak to Caipri directly. Her concentration was broken with a clack on her window. She looked around and saw Scion waving madly in her direction, then motioning for her to come and meet with him. Caipri smiled and rolled her eyes. She began to exit her cotoom and Olicai squawked at her in disapproval and shook his head.

"You are welcome to come with me if you wish."

Olicai blinked and tilted his head for a moment, as if to think carefully about her proposal, and then he laid his head back down. He squawked his protest but unwilling to get up at this hour. Caipri then made her way out of her dorsa to see what Scion was up to this time.

"Scion, what in Takenna's name are you doing?"

"My lady, my Sesuna." He bowed quickly and then sprang back upright. "I have come to inquire, that is if I could, that you come with me so I can show you... something."

"Something?" Caipri's ears pricked and her head tilted with the question.

"Yes, 'something.' I cannot say what it is as it is a surprise. I found it on one of my explorations and thought you would like to see it."

"Scion, you know I cannot leave Prima Dair until the Goddess calls me. My color will be seen."

"By nima light, Caipri - I mean, Sesuna- your color will not be seen." Scion held out his paw in anticipation.

Caipri looked up at the nima and then down and Scion's paw. She outreached her paw to his and she could see that by night their color was almost the same. She clasped his paw and looked at him with hesitation, Scion's soft gaze staring into her soul.

"Come, before someone sees us."

The pair sneaked through dorsas and avoided being seen by others in the tribe, then they headed North. Scion held on to Caipri's paw and guided her through the darkness, through the Kaian and out of Prima Dair. Once outside of the confines, their pace slowed as Scion continued to direct them on the exploration.

Caipri had never ventured outside of the Kaian and

suddenly she gasped in wander. Though it was dark, light was visible all around them. The sparkling sky above sent a calm pulsing through her veins as it mimicked the shine of her fur, and for the first time she felt as if she belonged. Peppulas and trees that during oreon light were a simple color, now in nima light shimmered and glowed. Grass tips shined like light upon the shaken water. As the wind passed through the land, the kiss of air made the light glow brighter on the foliage. Plants that were hidden by oreon light, rounded on top and sticking up above the ground, glowed in yellows, greens, and bright white. They were clumped together, shining in unison in all varying heights and top shapes from tall and pointy to short and stubby. All around were other specks of light, appearing to dance in the air and flit about in all directions. She reached out to touch one of these specks, but it darted away quickly. The speed of the retreat spooked Caipri and she clutched to Scion's arm.

"Scion, what are those?"

"Oh, those are lanarai. They glow at night and tend to stay away from the tribe as they are frightened by our size. I have slowly gained their trust while being out at Mizon Creek and they showed me the place where we are going. They may only look like tiny lights, but they have such a sense of humor." Scion laughed while thinking about conversations he had held with his little friends.

As if on cue, the lanarai flew upward in unison and created an illuminated path of light shining from above. Caipri's heart raced with anticipation and excitement as Scion led her through the land. Beginning to wonder what other things, or beings, dwelled within Ocaia had Caipri's mind all in a tangle. She knew she was about to get a glimpse of said wonders, but then knowing her fate to travel to the Eye of Takenna weighed heavily on her heart. She looked down at her hooves as she walked for a moment, and then lifted her eyes to take in the beauty of the nightscape. It was too amazing to simply let it slip her by in remorse for her future.

After traversing the grasslands, Scion gently guided her over the rocks in Mizon Creek, diligent to make sure she didn't lose her hoofing. It was not a wide creek, but with the Sesuna's sheltered life she was not an outdoorsy one and would require a little extra assistance. As expected, Caipri lost her hoofing on the last rock and fell straight into Scion's arms on the creek side. He pulled her up and over into the grass on the other side.

"Careful, Sesuna," he said with boisterous laughter. "I cannot bring you back to Prima Dair wet and dirty. The tribal elders will have me exiled."

Caipri met with Scion's eyes while grasping onto his arms, and for a moment... then she stood and brushed off her bluish fur promptly. "Thank you, Scion, but I had it managed."

"I know you did, Sesuna." Scion winked, a smile on his face that turned with him as he whipped around and continued their evening quest.

The lighted path began to dull as fewer lighted lanarai graced the sky above. Scion quickly trotted up a small hill and stopped. He turned to Caipri, adventurous excitement written into his eyes and a dim light cascaded over his nose. Difficult to make out the details behind him through the edge of darkness, but Caipri could see the 'something' was large and over the hill. Her pace quickened as she clambered up the greens to arrive at the peak next to Scion. Her breath stilled in awe as she attempted to sum up the large object in front of them.

"Are you ready?"

Caipri didn't feel ready, but she had come this far and didn't want to return alone. No. She had come to see 'something', and she was going to see it up close. She nodded and took Scion's outstretched paw once more to walk down the hill to see this discovery. With less lanarai to shed light on the details, she allowed her other senses to heighten and calm her conscious into knowing everything would be alright.

In front of them was a large structure, not a tree like anything known to their tribe. It towered higher toward the nima, covered in peppulas. It looked bent and broken, shapes that appeared like a dorsa window only much bigger and more beautiful than anything she had seen within Prima Dair. It was as long as it was tall with vines coming off the flat and chipped top. Broken pieces from the 'something' lay next to it in chunks. Caipri reached out and gently touched the side of it's beaten appearance. It was hard and solid like a boulder, and chilled to the touch.

"What is it?"

"I'm not sure. The lanarai brought me here and at first my mind was blown. I had never heard or seen any of the ancient writings tell of this 'something' before. And yes, before you ask, I went back and reviewed the writings to make sure and found nothing."

They stood in silence, gazing at the marvel before them for several moments. Not only had Caipri broken every rule of exiting Prima Dair before her time, she was now standing in the midst of a completely new object that no one else seemed to know about.

Caipri broke the silence. "So, what now?"

"What now? Well, don't you think we should tell the tribe?"

"And then what, Scion? I'm not supposed to be out of Prima Dair, let alone discovering a new 'something' that rewrites our Takenna Life."

Her chiding words hit Scion deeply. She was right of course. It was a mistake to bring her to this discovery knowing that Caipri would soon travel to the Eye of Takenna to fulfill her duties as Sesuna. As his paw rested on the face of the artifact, he gathered his thoughts and contemplated his Takenna Life. Caipri was seemingly doing the same thing. Scion looked at her, noticing the wonder in her eyes as she gazed over the large object, and could not stop himself from speaking boldly.

"Run away with me."

Caipri shook her head in disbelief. "Do what?"

"Run away with me."

She scoffed her breath with an attempt of laughter to

his proposal. Unfortunately, it was a failed attempt and her mind suddenly latched onto the possibility of escaping her life sentence of devotion and solitude. Caipri looked at Scion, noting that this time his face was written with a solemn and serious expression that she had never seen on him before. She was utterly speechless. Scion took her paws, gently caressing them within his own while balancing between looking at her and her paws.

"Caipri, my Sesuna, listen." He closed his eyes, then opened them and looked in her eyes with such intent that he had never mustered the courage to do. "I love you, and I have always loved you. If you do travel to the Eye of Takenna as is your birth right, I do not know what I'll do with the void in my heart. This 'something' means there could be more out there in Ocaia. I cannot explain why, but I feel that my place in Takenna's Life is drawing me outward from the tribe and with a different purpose. I want to see what else is out there, and I want you there with me. I want you in my future gean."

Still speechless, Caipri's thoughts whirled in a million different directions while playing many scenarios in her head. While Scion patiently awaited a response, Caipri's heart throbbed within her chest and her stomach turned. Finally, she agreed with herself the appropriate response to make. She, and the entire tribe, knew of Scion's feelings for her but she never thought he would actually confess his affection.

"Scion, you are one of Takenna's special servants of Ocaia. Perhaps you are called to seek these new discoveries, but my place is Sesuna. I must maintain my duty to the Goddess of Life and travel to the Eye of Takenna when I am called. We all have our place in Takenna's Life."

In a respective manner, and without missing a step, Scion bowed his forehead to touch Caipri's paw.

"Let's get you back to your dorsa, Sesuna."

Caipri's body ached with his respectful response, but Scion gently guided her back to Prima Dair under the glowing light of the lanarai. She was more careful this time on the rocks at Mizon Creek and did not want a repeat of holding onto Scion once more. They slowly made their way back to the Kaian, but this time they did not have to dodge the eyes of tribe members as most of them were now in their dorsas.

Arriving at Caipri's dorsa, Scion stood back and kept his distance out of respect. Caipri stopped when she got to the door and turned to him.

"Thank you, Scion. I appreciated your company."

Scion bowed at his Sesuna and replied, "The pleasure was all mine."

Caipri retreated to her dorsa, and Scion retreated to his. He replayed the events of the nima light and tried to figure out if he could have done or said anything differently for her to see that her life was more than service to the Goddess.

Caipri entered her dorsa to an upset midawal and padiwal, and Olicai was sitting on the table with what looked a face of "I told you so."

"I have been worried sick! Where have you been off to?" Taltaira appeared frantic with her paw fingers twisting within each other, and Gaitartuwain sat stone-faced in his chair.

"I was just out with a friend, Midawal. I'm sorry but neither of you were home when I returned from my nightly Takenna prayer."

Taltaira placed her paws on her haunches. "Well, as Sesuna, we have to ensure your safety. I'm just glad that you are back and in one piece as Takenna intended. We found Olicai by himself and you never leave him behind unless he is resting." Caipri's midawal, Taltaira, was just over her prime age and still stood like a young-aged palawal lady. Her size was average, but her eyes had a hint of green that most others in the village did not possess.

"Olicai was resting, and I offered for him to accompany me, but he laid back down." Caipri shot him a dirty stare when her midawal was not looking in her direction.

Caipri and Taltaira clasped paws and smiled at each other in unison. This was quickly interrupted with Padiwal's insertion. He stood, growing tall and for a not-so-fierce creature, looked terrifying with his deep and brooding brown eyes. He was one of the tallest males in the tribe, and his hooves more massive in size than his cohorts. Gaitartuwain was revered. Scars covered his body from years of working on tools that made Prima Dair so successful in recent oreon cycles.

"Rumor spread that Scion was also absent from his dorsa. You were not out this nima with that misfit, were you?"

"Padiwal, please," Caipri swiped her paw in his direction to pass off his statement. "Scion has done his best to charm me, but my duty is to Takenna. I am Sesuna. I know better."

Padiwal's stare felt puncturing to Caipri's soul. She held her stance, assured in her response and ability to hide where she had been under the nima sky. After a moment, he nodded and retreated to his cotoom. Caipri and Taltaira nodded to each other, signaling it was time to rest for all of them.

Once her in cotoom, she looked out her window once more and stared at the Fountain of Takenna. Caipri could not unsee the 'something' that Scion had led her to. Caipri then turned her attention to Olicai.

"Traitor."

He looked at her, flipped his beak upward and turned around showing his long, white tail feathers in Caipri's direction.

"Really? You're mad at me?"

Olicai slightly looked at her from the side, and then turned his beak away and back up in the air. His protest was adorable and Caipri held back her laughter.

"I didn't leave you for long. How could I do that to my best friend? Do you think you could forgive me?" Caipri outstretched her arms, waiting to hug her bird.

He slowly turned, still holding a slight look of protest. Then he jumped into her arms and nestled into her neck.

"I knew you couldn't stay mad at me. Tell you what, you can come next time."

Olicai squawked, flapped his wings and nodded.

Scion felt restless in his resting bunk as he recounted his adventure with Caipri. Tossing and turning in the darkness, his dreams took an unfamiliar turn into lands of the unseen. Paw fingers swayed from side to side as he walked forward, sight pivoted in all directions while taking in the landscape. Open, wide lands of orange grass that were bordered by tall, red trees. The vision was hazy, and the sense of smell was nonexistent.

Suddenly a new form was in view, but difficult to make out through the blurred picture in his mind. A blue Dolgaian appeared and was speaking, but while the mouth was moving no sound emitted. Confused, Scion tried to speak but he could not hear the words he was attempting to make. The creature before him laughed, or looked to have laughed, at what he had said… but how could that be?

He shook his head trying to make sense of his surroundings, then turned his attention in another direction. Oreon was high in the East and appeared to be near midday as they continued to walk Eastward. The vast land went on as far as the eye could see and a band of water crossed the horizon with mountains peeking behind it. The Savidi Mor was approaching, and he laid his paw on top of a marker to catch his breath at the marvelous sight. A deep feeling of calm and resolve caressed his soul as he knew that he would be returning soon.

Eastern Discovery

Several oreon and nima cycles passed since Scion and Caipri had their adventure. Deep inside, a tug of hope held on that perhaps she would change her mind and be in his gean. As the warm light fell each day and nima's light glimmered on the paths of Prima Dair, he waited by the Fountain of Takenna. Well, he waited some of the day any way. There was much to explore, and while he desired to be with Caipri, the un-discovered world of Ocaia beckoned him forth during oreon light to search for such exploits.

On this day, he would travel to the East and South of his favorite Mizon Creek. He gathered his tarp and tack, then exited out of his dorsa. Although no words were exchanged, he could feel the deep and utter anger radiating from Jiana onto his back as he left. Looking around the Kaian at the local faces, wandering to and fro in their meager lives and assimilation construct to the tribe, he shrugged off the ties that felt binding to him and went about his way.

This new track took him through some treed areas of light-colored purple, leaves longer bladed and sharing peppulas of pale yellow. Scion stared for a moment, as he had not seen a tree like this before. Almost as long as the grass beneath his hooves, the purple leaves flowed from their high stature and nearly kissed his nose. Yellow peppulas, small and graceful, placed at the roots of these leaves, were also longer in length with their petals and had clear budding

laces that rose from the center. A curious encounter, Scion slowly approached the tree to gaze closer at the new peppula. Gently in the breeze, the petals and leaves danced from side to side and unleashed a very tart smell. Immediately, Scion covered his nose and started scoffing at the stench that just rendered him nauseas.
 "What in Takenna's name?! Ugh!"
 Scion coughed and batted at his nose to try and rid the smell faster. It burned the inside of his nostrils and no attempt to rid himself of it was helpful. After composing himself, he stood and stared at the beautiful tree - both with disdain and appreciation. Not that he may need it, but it was a mental note he made that in case of emergency, he should bring any foe near this dangerous tree. However, second note, do not breathe while passing beneath it.
 By this time, oreon was about to kiss the Eastern horizon. He continued on and steered clear of those bunch of trees when he came upon a hill that was covered in peppulas of more shades and sizes than he had ever seen. Tales were told of Takenna's colors, not blue like her Chosen Palawals, but the other ranging colors of her every essence. Some colors were seen in Prima Dair, but these before him were brighter and more full of Takenna's Life. They all varied, even among the ones that appeared similar, Scion could see they were not exactly identical. Petals were rounded, cut, and tapered in every color he found. Each main color had an internal color budding from the center that did not match another. Compliment

that with the varying types of petals and this was truly something to admire. He ran through the peppulas on the hill, bounding from one patch to another, investigating and looking to find a matching pair. What a discovery!

As he marveled in the bask of Takenna's Life and glory, he turned his gaze to the East again and over the hill. He squinted as the oreon light made it difficult to focus through the light coming back into his eyes. Unable to see clearly, he made his way down the hill and noticed the footing underneath his hooves started to give way. Unable to catch his balance, he tripped and rolled down the hill several times over before he reached the bottom of the hill. He shook off the stumble and spat out something distasteful in his mouth. When spitting did not work, he grabbed his tongue and tried to pry off the nasty bits still inside. He paused when he realized he could finally see the landscape that had drawn him closer as the light was not projected from oreon so brightly at this angle.

As far as his keen eyes could see, a land of brown and no trees or peppulas. He could see some rise and fall to the land, but it seemed uninhabited by any creature - known or unknown. His ears pricked up to detect signs of life, or danger, but only the breeze caught within. He noticed the air was dull, no sign of sweetness like in Prima Dair, and his nose tensed with the lack of such sweet air to which he was accustomed.

He took a few steps forward, sinking in his movement as the land gave way under hoof. Scion looked down and saw no green, and he bent down to feel this strange terrain. He plucked up a bit of the new 'something' and it disintegrated between his paw fingers. His head twitched from side to side as he watched it float down and back from whence it came. As he stood and gathered the thoughts in his mind, his tail swished from side to side with curiosity.

Satisfied that he had seen enough, he looked back up the hill he had fallen from. I hope I can make it back up. He turned and made an agonizing way back up the hill, getting stuck and yet slipping at the same time with each step he made. Once he reached the summit, he rolled into the peppulas he had previously left behind and laid among them for a moment.

Regaining his breath, Scion stood on the hill and took in the sight of "home." Prima Dair was one of many regions, and none ventured further than needed. The market share between his land and Joto was to the South, and none had ever mentioned the sights that he had seen today. Seeing that oreon had almost completely receded for the evening and nima was in the sky, he set up for a night in the wild and hoped that his gean wouldn't worry too much while he was away.

As oreon graced the sky with wisps of orange and pink clouds, Scion awoke feeling rather sore but refreshed at the same time. He stretched his limbs but noticed an ache in his hooves, then rolled himself to his stomach to push himself up and make the brisk walk back to Prima Dair. As he continued to stretch, he looked around at the landscape and marveled at the peppulas. Stunning. Scion knew better than to try again to woo Caipri with another bouquet. However, he was known for his stubborn attitude. He decided to pick brighter and more exotic peppulas to show Caipri this time. These were not your ordinary peppulas, these were from the East and even if she was to hold her duty to Takenna, he wanted to share this discovery with her. After all, he had already shown her the first of his discoveries and she appeared to be fascinated.

A chill air wafted through Scion's fur and made his skin shudder. The changing of the oreon could sometimes feel bitter, making him appreciate the warmth of the air now leaving its time in Ocaia. This was the time when Prima Dair made a last bit of effort to gather and farm as much as they could to carry them through the cold days. Although he liked his freedom, if the Dolgaian could not survive on their harvest then none would awaken to the warmer suns of oreon.

◆ ◆ ◆

The long and brisk walk back to Prima Dair made Scion feel more weak and tired this day. He chalked it up to be that steep hill he had to climb up, which had never happened before and took quite a bit of hoof-work. The peppulas he found, though, were well worth his exploration today and proved to him that he found his path in Ocaia. Scion made his way through the Kaian and to the Fountain.

Caipri was in the middle of her nightly praise, Olicai by her side, and she caught Scion out of her peripheral. She didn't want to anger Takenna but tried to hurry the nightly song before Scion had a chance to speak with her. While her heart and mind were conflicted, speaking to him would make matters worse. She was unable to pray fast enough and Scion appeared behind her. She quickly called for Olicai to come and turned away from Scion.

"Sesuna, wait!"

Caipri could not disregard the request of the tribe when called. Sutanai sensi she whispered to herself as she turned to face Scion.

"Yes, Scion?"

Scion approached and bowed, and Olicai quickly stepped between them. The two had a slight standoff as Olicai knew when Caipri did not want to be bothered. White tail feathers began to rise in the air, a sign of caution to the intruder, and beady eyes narrowed as the bird crossed in front of the Sesuna.

"Olicai, please. I brought something for you too." Scion pulled out a wiggle bug, fresh from the ground on his way back to Prima Dair. He was prepared for Olicai, knowing that he was generally close behind Caipri.

Olicai squawked, lowered his tail feathers, and focused on the snack in Scion's paws. He squawked again and Scion tossed it to him. A devious smirk crossed Scion's face and then he proceeded to continue his discussion with Caipri.

"Sesuna, I was traveling East and found these peppulas. They were on a large hill and, from what I could tell, none were the same. See? These colors, and shapes, they are all different. These are unlike anything we see in Prima Dair and I thought you would like to have them."

Scion presented the bouquet to her after fidgeting with them to show the color of the petals. Caipri's eyes grew large with confusion, excitement, or was it sheer wonder? She snatched the bouquet from him, continuing his prior fidgeting as she too was looking through them and saw that none was a match to another. This was truly remarkable! She looked at him, her breath increasing in pace as her heart began to race eagerly, and she was speechless for a moment.

"These are - beautiful."

A smile graced both of their faces. She knew that this was another discovery that he had made and shared it with her. He knew that she was not supposed to show him affection, and yet she was doing it.

"Perhaps, someday, I can show them to you on the hill?" Scion could not help himself in asking.

As Caipri looked at him, the smile retracted and her eyes gave way to become more riddled with sadness. Her gaze then turned to the bunch of peppulas and she sniffed them gently as her mind wheeled with determining an answer. She had said once that her duty was to Takenna, and it was, but such a lonely life existed in her destiny. Caipri looked back up at Scion and was about to speak when a boisterous, nasally voice called out to them.

"Caipri, time for dinner," Taltaira called out to her.

They looked at each other, Scion hinging on a potential response. Caipri smiled back, curtsied, and turned to return to her dorsa with a quick reply.
"Thank you, Scion."

❖ ❖ ❖

"What are those?" Taltaira reached quickly at the bouquet with intensity that Caipri had never seen before.
"I'm not sure, Midawal. Scion found them today. Something about 'traveling East.'"
"Well, I have never seen the likes of these beauties before. East, you say? Not sure what lies out that way, but these are truly a sight to see of Takenna's Life."
Taltaira fetched a holding tin and water for the new peppulas, then placed them on the table. Other bouquets that had been given to Caipri were never displayed in the main dorsa living quarters. Luckily, Padiwal was not yet home and, in their hearts, they hoped he would not throw them out upon arrival. Gifts came plenty to their family as Caipri was the Sesuna, being a Chosen Palawal of Takenna was a gift itself and the tribe felt pleasure in showering their gean with trinkets in Takenna's favor.
Caipri knew that Scion was different. His trinkets and bouquets were not shown in an attempt to bring himself higher in Takenna's favor. Scion would rather see her happy with him than devote her life to

Takenna in solitude at the temple. His persistence was at first bothersome, and try as she might to fight him and protest, Scion continued to show his affection. She also knew that his use of 'Sesuna' was to ensure that he showed his respect, but he had called her Caipri by accident on numerous occasions. Why couldn't the rest of the tribe treat her more like 'Caipri' and less like 'Sesuna?' Just thinking about it made her heart skip a beat.

Taltaira and Caipri prepared dinner when Gaitartuwain entered the dorsa. He knocked off the dirt from his hooves and then made his way to the table. Set to eat, they all gathered around and gave praise to Takenna before breaking honey tarfe.

"What.. are.. those?" Gaitartuwain's tone was deep and suspicious.

"Aren't they lovely, dear? Young Scion found these today and brought them back to Caipri." Taltaira boasted as if the bouquet had been given to her. Probably for the best, anything from Scion rubbed Padiwal the wrong way.

"Why are they all - er - different?" Gaitartuwain's confusion led to a tilt of the head and some crumbs falling from his mouth.

Caipri interjected before Midawal said something too confounding, "Well, he doesn't know. He said he found them on a hill to the East while traveling, and he brought them back to show me and noted that all of them are different colors, sizes, and shapes. He said the entire hill looked like that, with not two peppulas looking the same. Can you believe that?" She faux laughed off the explanation and then she shoved tarfe in her mouth. Gaitartuwain shrugged and continued to eat.

  After dinner, Caipri and her family retreated to their cotooms. As nightly ritual, Caipri went to the window and gazed at the Fountain of Takenna. She had noticed Scion sitting there on the edge at night since their adventure, but she was too afraid to go to him or let herself be seen in the night. Almost certain, Caipri judged the nightly standoff as a way to lure her back out to seek a new discovery under the cover of nima light. It might not have been, but Scion was definitely persistent and cunning. She wanted to go on another adventure, see new things outside of Prima Dair and live a life of freedom such as Scion. Duty to her Goddess, to her gean, was a weight she had to carry out of tradition. As expected, he was there at the edge of the Fountain. Caipri's heart rate spiked and her breath became stiff at the sight of Scion. Her mind and her heart played games with each other, snagging back and forth between what was real and what could not be.

  Caipri looked down and inspected her paw fingers, with deep purple hue, and clutched them into a fist. Tears welled in her eyes, fell down her cheeks, and landed onto her fists. All of this duty felt unbearable, but there was no escaping her fate.

◆ ◆ ◆

Scion could see Caipri in her window, looking down and appearing dismayed. It was difficult to see inside exactly what was happening, but he could tell a distraught face when he saw it. He trotted to the window and knocked gently to get her attention. Startled, she looked up quickly and wiped away tears from her cheeks. They smirked at one another in the awkward encounter, and he waved her outside to come speak with him.

Caipri exited the dorsa, Olicai following close behind this time, and made her way to the Kaian. She was twisting her paw fingers in her fur to the side but stood tall and proud before Scion.

"Are you alright, Cai -" Scion coughed and reworded himself, "Are you alright, Sesuna?"

Caipri held her stance and laughed, "Yes, of course I'm alright."

Each of them stood a distance from each other, silent and waiting for the other to speak. Awkwardly, Olicai stood to the side of them and stared at one and then the other, waiting for them to speak as well and confused why no one was talking to him specifically. After a moment, Caipri walked to the Fountain and sat on the edge in her usual song sitting spot. Nima light made her twinkle on the edge of her fur, life breathed into her essence in the darkness and Scion found her to be truly a beautiful member of the tribe. Duty or no duty to Takenna, he wanted to at least be a confidant to his Sesuna. He neared her, but kept a slight distance, and stood before his love in solidarity to whatever woes she held.

"Sesuna, you are free to speak with me if you wish. You can be Takenna assured that nothing you say will leave this mouth." Scion made a sweeping gesture across his face and then tucked his paws behind him, as if to suggest he was a troop and sworn to service like Caipri.

"Oh, Scion," she mustered a mild giggle. "You are free. Free to discover, do what you want, go where you wish without being stopped," then her voice trailed off into a whisper, "to love whom you want."

Tears began to well again in her eyes though she tried to fight them back. Olicai stood by her legs and placed his head on her hooves to comfort her.

Scion knelt beside Caipri and took her paw. His eyes focused on her paw, not her eyes for he could not bear to see her this way. He knew not what it was like to look different and held to such a high standard within Ocaia. A Chosen Palawal of Takenna was supposed to be a gift, and yet, he saw it was less a gift and more of a death sentence. He clutched her paws, shut his eyes tightly, and tried to find the words inside to sooth her soul and let her know that everything would be alright.

"Sesuna, I cannot comprehend the struggle that you must face. Duty to the Goddess of Life and being gifted with her grace and hue. What I do feel is that we all have a choice. A choice to be what Takenna calls us for, not just what the tribe tells us to be true."

Their eyes met. Caipri was shocked at his response and it was far from anything ever said for a Sesuna or

Sesuni to decide their destiny. None had ever tried to defy their nature and made their journey to the Eye of Takenna when called. Caipri pulled her paw away from his grasp in her confusion and from the mountain of emotions piling on at once. Can I change my destiny?

"Scion, I appreciate that your wanderlust has provided you with a new outlook on your Takenna Life. My place is where my Goddess takes me." Caipri stood and scurried back into her dorsa, Olicai trotting close behind, and left Scion alone with his own thoughts.

Looking at the Fountain of Takenna, Scion gave praise to his Goddess and then sought her guidance. "Takenna, please, show me my path. How can you put Caipri before me just to take her away?"

Scion stared at the stone Goddess for a moment, waiting for her answer. Each second that passed was a sting in his heart as he felt conflicted by the path laid before him and Caipri. He slowly shook his head, ears drooped with despair, and stood next to the fountain as he continued to wonder what his Takenna Life would be. Scion gazed back up to the Goddess' face, nima light twinkling in his amber eyes as tears began to swell. He tapped the side of the fountain with his paw fingers before retreating to his dorsa.

Another upsetting encounter with Caipri edged into Scion's slumber. He wrestled with the emotions flowing through him and wrapped in his unwavering ability to let her go. Peaceful dreams of wandering Ocaia as a free Dolgaian were interrupted again and picked up where the last odd dream left off.

He picked up his paw from the marker and stood up straight, swinging a blade over his shoulder. A deep inhale inflated his lungs, and still no smell could be detected. Scion turned his attention to the blue Dolgaian as the member slapped his shoulder with a smile. The embrace felt comforting to his soul, although he did not feel his touch. The vision was blurred as before, watching the blue form walk ahead as two more Dolgaian males made stride behind him. Scion followed suit, holding his head up with pride and ears upright. Elation of the sight before him and knowing the journey will soon be over.

What journey will soon be over?

The Dolgaian pressed forward and made light discussion as they continued toward the Savidi Mor. Words were lightly making their way to Scion's ears, but he could not make them out. As his sight was hindered, so were the scents and hearing. Senses were not functioning, but he kept up his gait with the other members. Scion continued to watch the Sesuni ahead, it could not be any other Dolgaian based on the hue of his fur.

At last, the troop reached the Savidi Mor and took a break on the Western bank. Conversation continued as they opened tarps and ate tarf in the grass. Suddenly, Scion's ears twitched as if he had heard something coming but he didn't actually hear it. He stood up on his hooves quickly as he scanned through the hazy picture of the Savidi Mor. Then he saw something moving in the water...

An Unwelcomed Encounter

A muddled mind clouded Scion as he awoke to the bright oreon light that crept into his window. He turned his body away from the window, shielding him from the new day that pressed upon him. His dreams grew increasingly more detailed, and left him with more questions than answers. Those images on top of his continuous strain to hold on to Caipri made him feel that he was in need of stretching his hooves further than before, as least within comfort. He reluctantly rose from his resting bunk and proceeded to head into the main room to gather his tarp. He found Jiana making tarfe, as usual, with his midawal sitting silently at the table.

"Good oreon, Midawal." Scion walked over to her and touched her paw as he spoke, then turned to his sister to politely address her as well. "Jiana."

"Scion," Shawartia stated in a low and raspy voice, "what will you get up to today?"

He huffed a small laugh as he looked upon her whitening fur and light-hearted, squinty eyes. "I do not know yet, Midawal. I feel that my hooves need to seek new land to trod upon and I will go where Takenna takes me."

"Takenna guides us, my palawal. Smart of you to remember this." Shawartia pointed a shaky and wrinkled paw finger at her palawal as she spoke. A smile peeked across her face as she continued, "Your Padiwal was very fond of traveling South, toward Joto. I never made the journey to market with him, but he said the trees and peppulas were so radiant and beautiful. He would bring me peppulas after his travel, you know. He also told me about the Tricornia, watching them frolic in the lands in the nima light."

Jiana abruptly inserted, "Midawal, Tricornia are not real. Those are palawal stories."

"No," Shawartia insisted, "no, my sweet, they are real. I have never gazed upon them with my own two eyes, but Sciotain would not have been untruthful to me. He saw them," she exclaimed and tapped her paw fist on the table. She then turned her unfocused gaze in Scion's direction, "Your padiwal told me that he saw them running across the open land, under the light of a large nima, with young ones following behind. Grazing they were, on the grass that leads to the Joto market. You should see such beauty of Takenna's creation while you still breathe and live within her realm."

Scion grabbed his midawal's paws within his. "I do not intend to be out passed the nima rise, but I do hope to be able to see the Tricornia someday."

Jiana rolled her eyes and continued to press her tarfe paste. Shawartia's face crinkled up with a wide grin as she shook Scion's paws.

Scion continued, "Well, I am off. I do not know where, but as I stated, I will be back before nima rises." With that, he turned on his hooves, swung his tarp over his shoulder and headed out of the dorsa.

The Kaian was bustling with activity. The female Dolgaian that fashioned garb and wear for others were showing their finest new trends, made of the twigs and field leftovers to make beautiful neck lacings, paw danglers, and haunch sashes. Some creators were better than others, and it was well known which of them had better paw fingers to make such draping. As Scion wandered through and made his way South, he crossed in front of Maichin and his gean dorsa. A fine display of neck lacings was there, and one had caught the eye of Scion.

"Good oreon, Maichin. Say, this one is just beautiful. Your midawal still has an amazing touch."

"Thank you, Scion!" Maichin, grabbed the neck lacing to show to his potential customer. "Midawal took these twigs from the trees by the Eastern rim, but these seeds of shining pink were found under the Western rim trees. The leaves are from the trees of Joto, the orange hues compliment the colors of both regions."

The pitch was nice, and Scion could not help but think of how beautiful it would look around Caipri's neck. Her deep purple and light blue fur would complete the look nicely. "This is incredible. Tell you what, Jiana is working on a new batch of tarfe today so if you let me have this neck lacing then we will barter you two servings of tarfe."

Maichin had a great smile on his face, his deep brown eyes disappearing as his cheeks grew up into them. "Deal! When shall we pick up the tarfe?"

"Later today. Jiana should be done with your batch as oreon is highest in the sky." Scion took the neck lacing and placed in within his tarp as he continued to speak.

"Thank you, Scion. Takenna provides."

Scion waved quickly as he walked away, continuing to the South. "Takenna provides."

He knew Jiana was going to be furious with him when she heard the news that two servings of her tarfe was now spoken for, but he thought it was well worth it. The gift was tucked away as he made his venture, following along the beaten path toward Joto. Scion had no intention of going to market with their Southern neighbor, but he hoped that something would pique his interest on the way and lead him on a new discovery. Finding the large structure to the North and East of Prima Dair created a pulse in his soul that he could not hold down. He longed for more intrigue in his regular life and would not give up the drive to seek out more.

His hooves carried him through the tall grasslands of Prima Dair and led out of his familiar land. He stopped and gazed about him, noticing the change of colors coming about in reds and oranges. Midawal's earlier story was beginning to play out, with peppulas taking on new shapes and colors. He could see how Padiwal would have found interest in this place and bringing a piece of it back to share with her. As he surveyed around him, studying the sway of the grass, scent in the air, he noticed to the West that there were some mountains on the other side of the tree line. He squinted and put a paw above his brow to get an idea of how far the mountains were. The Tuskula Mountains, said to bridge the path between the land and waters of the Pati Maio, were not as tall as he had though based on the stories he heard as a palawal. Scion decided in an instant that he was going to at least see the base of the mountains, knowing that going too deep would leave him stranded and alone.

  Course laid in, Scion grabbed his tarp with one paw and strode his hooves to the West. Vibrant flowers were hidden deep in the tall grass, and Scion took notice of them below his hooves. He gazed over them as he crossed, attempting to not disturb them as best as he could. Trees grew closer, large with lustrous leaves of long blades and orange in color. Oreon shining upon them gave the leaves a twinkle of light, dancing in the breeze that wafted through them. As Scion neared the trees, he noticed that they were massive in size and much larger than he had anticipated at his original distance. The trunks were thick, twisted, and the branches nearly as thick as they came up and then down with heavy bladed leaves. He stood and stared upward at the trees for a moment, taking in their majesty.

  Then, Scion looked forward into the forest. Dark behind the leaves, an unknown world lay beyond its cover and he felt ready to take on a new challenge. He took a quick, deep breath and then pressed forward as he exhaled. He pushed the long leaves aside with his paws and peered around them as he walked through the darkness. It was not completely dark with oreon light coming through the tops of the trees and dotting a path forward for him. After a few paces, he decided that he need to chart his course in case he got lost and needed to find his way back. He broke a small branch from a tree, thinking that the broken branches would be an identifiable way to return, when he heard a deep rumbling noise coming from behind him. He turned slowly, back now facing the broken branch, and stared into the dark wood. The fur on his back and tail were standing straight up on heightened alert as he felt something was amiss but could not see anything coming toward him. Rustling sounds took place around him, he would turn his focus to each side where sound was emitting, and his large ears were standing straight up.

Scion then realized that he was unarmed, holding only a tarp to carry things of his intrigue. He began to walk backward, toward the edge of the trees from where he entered, and was met by a creature he had never seen, or heard of, before. He looked upon a reddish-brown beast, with orange and yellow stripes dripping down its back. Scion stopped and stared, unsure of what to do, and the large creature stared back as it crept forward. Large paws disturbed the fallen leaves below, and a fierce face emerged that bore large teeth, two protruding from its mouth and hooking backward, and horns upon either brow. Narrowed eyes, outlined in black, were stark yellow like the oreon in the sky and felt as though they were peering into Scion's soul.

"Intruder." The beast snarled as it made its way into the spotted light. The nose was broad, and long, but the creature's ears were rather small compared to Scion's.

"I am not an intruder. I am a humble explorer, come

to see the beautiful lands of Joto." Scion nervously continued conversation as he was contemplating his way out of this mess.

"You are not familiar. Who are you?"

"My name is Scion. I mean you no harm."

The beast scoffed. "You would not be able to do me harm even if you wished." It continued to creep forward, large paws growing larger as they grew nearer and now Scion could also see a long tail swinging behind it.

"Of course I could not harm you," Scion continued. "You are the fiercest of creatures in Ocaia. There is no way I would win against you."

Confused, the fiendish animal stopped and stared hard into Scion's eyes. "You do not fear me?"

"Fear is such a strong word." While Scion did, in this moment, fear the creature he could not let on that he felt such emotion. Nervously, Scion came up with something more suitable for this situation. "Revere, I revere you."

"What is revere?"

"I admire you, adore you, think of you as being superior. Takenna surely knew what she was doing when she created your kind." Scion was scrambling for words to buy time as he was slowly making his way back to open land.

"I am the leader of the Natiko. Jantu is my name, and I am the strongest of Takenna's palawals." The beast stood proud, light cascading on its face and highlighting the colors of its fur. Blended colors camouflaged into the trees and leaves, which now made Scion understand how he had not spotted him before.

"Natiko, yes. Our ancestors wrote of your magnificence." Scion was steadily backing up, grasping at any magnificent lie he could conjure to get him out of this encounter. "It was said that you can sneak between the trees without being seen."

The eyes of Jantu softened as he was being flattered, and the claws began to retreat slightly. Scion could see that he was making progress in this scuffle and hoped for a Takenna miracle to get him out of this one.

"You have heard of me? How interesting, considering that I have never heard of you." Jantu took a large step forward, "What are you?"

Scion continued to back up as he spoke, trying to not make it too obvious. "Oh me? I am just a Dolgaian of Prima Dair."

"Prima Dair? Dwellers of Prima Dair do not come here." Jantu stepped forward, and Scion stepped back at the same pace. "Dolgaian. You do not appear to be very strong to me." Jantu's tail began to waft the leaves behind him as he prowled forward, a sign that made Scion increasingly uneasy.

"Not strong, no. We are... simple creatures. We make food for ourselves and create neck lacings to wear. I can show you one, if you wish."

"Neck lacing? What is a neck lacing?"

Scion stuck out a paw, to indicate for Jantu to pause his pursuit, then he knelt down and removed the tarp from his shoulder. He reached into the tarp, causing the Natiko to tense slightly and expose the teeth within his mouth, and Scion pulled out the neck lacing he bartered from Maichin earlier. It dangled from Scion's paw fingers, glistening in the faint oreon light coming through the treetops, and Jantu's expression suddenly changed to fascination.

"Neck lacing?"

Scion slowly stood as he held the item and replied, "Yes. My tribe makes these. Do you like it?"

Jantu's eyes grew wide and his face softened as he gently stepped forward. His tail swished behind him, but in a more playful manner than before. The difference of approach was exactly what Scion needed to make an escape.

"I see that you do like it. It goes around your neck, hence the name. Do you want it?"

"Indeed. I will take your neck lacing, and I will let you live."

Scion gulped as he responded, "That sounds like a fair trade. I will leave it here for you." Scion laid it down atop the leaves gently and continued to speak, "I thank you, Jantu, Leader of the Natiko. You have a great oreon and enjoy." He took a long bow and backed up as quickly as he could.

Once Scion was clear of the large trees, he sprinted on all fours back toward Prima Dair. The encounter was too close for comfort and it was time to seek refuge on familiar ground. As his hooves and paws dug through the tall grass, Scion heard a large roar coming from the wood behind him. Fur stood up on edge as he realized that the offering did not buy him enough time. Come on hooves! Scion shook his head and put all of his energy into running faster.

Leaves burst to the sides as Jantu emerged abruptly, searching the open land for his prey. Once his eyes adjusted to the bright light, he could see a patch of grass that was moving in a different pattern than the wind. Another deep roar echoed through the landscape and Jantu began his pursuit of Scion. Dirt kicked up under the large paws of Jantu, and his legs were longer than Scion's which made the chase more thrilling for the Natiko.

Scion gave his limbs all he could muster as he continued to head North and East, searching for his refuge. Jantu was hot on his hooves, heaving low and deep as he bounded over the land effortlessly. Scion never looked back, knowing it would not help to see the massive monster with his teeth and horns coming closer. He cut to the East, darting over a small hill and drawing his attacker after him. On the other side of the hill, Scion ran toward the trees with long, light-colored purple petals and wove in-between the tree gathering as large paws gained their distance. Suddenly, Scion was rolled over and pressed under those massive paws, claws on either side of his slender neck, as he stared up at his attacker.

Jantu huffed deeply, given the great chase that just ensued, and a satisfied smile grew upon his face. "Your neck lacing broke into pieces after you left. That piece of Dolgaian filth was useless and you knew it."

"No, you're mistaken, Leader of the Na-aghhh!"

Jantu put pressure on Scion's neck as he spoke, and an evil grimace rolled on his face as he pushed into his prey. "You cannot fool me. You only did this to save yourself, but you were still unable to do so."

As Scion gasped for breath, a long breeze made its appearance through the trees above. Scion held his short breath, closed his eyes, and waited for either the beast to kill him or the trees to run him back to his homeland. Jantu had wrath in his bright yellow eyes, when suddenly the Natiko's nostrils began to flair. Pressure released off Scion's neck as Jantu huffed and coughed under the wretched smell emitted from the trees around them. The Natiko roared and turned tail back to the trees near Joto, and Scion rolled onto his belly and crawled out of the unsavory trees. Fresh air finally drew into Scion's lungs as he hit the tall grass in the open land.

Regaining consciousness, and slowly expunging the dismal smell from his nasal passages, he looked back to the South and could not see Jantu any longer. Scion realized that he was ill prepared for such an encounter, save for the trees that fulfilled their duty at the perfect moment. He pushed himself up from the ground, taking in the last of oreon's light for the day, and looked North to Prima Dair. Hooves reset under his body and he made his way slowly back to the Kaian.

As nima rose in the sky, Scion walked through the Kaian and made his way to his dorsa. He walked through the door, stiff and unsettled with his day, to find Jiana and Shawartia at the table. Both females looked up from the table, albeit Shawartia's gaze was off focus, as Scion walked in.

"Scion. Jiana and I were just talking about you."

"Yes, Midawal," Jiana interrupted. "We were speaking about Maichin, and you, as you apparently made a barter today for a neck lacing. We humbly gave him the servings of tarfe, but where is this neck lacing?"

Scion bowed his head in shame. He did not account for the barter deal when he attempted to save his life. "I no longer have the neck lacing."

Jiana threw her paws in the air as she stood and walked to her cutting table. Shawartia reached out with her paw toward Scion, and he obliged her by taking it.

"Midawal, I am sorry. I had intended it as a gift for Caipri." Scion raised his gaze to Jiana and continued, "I had to then barter it to a Natiko, in exchange for my life. Even then, I barely survived."

Shawartia squeezed Scion's paw as she nodded and smiled, happy that her paliwal made it home safe. Meanwhile, Jiana was fuming on the other side of the small room and shook her head from side to side. Scion could tell that this was a major hit to their gean, bartering without fair trade.

"Why?" Jiana muttered, in nearly a whisper.

"I was going to give it to Caipri, as I stated previously."

Jiana turned her hefty body back toward them, staring down at Scion as she spoke. "Our tarfe is not for your gain of impression with the Sesuna. You are no longer allowed to barter our tarfe for your means. If you want to barter, then do so on your own." She slapped a paw on the table, staring eye-to-eye with her younger brother.

Scion nodded and his ears slunk back to his head with dismay. He squeezed his midawal's paw and made his exit to his cotoom without saying another word. As he entered his cotoom, he knew that what he had done was completely irresponsible. Not only had he jeopardized his gean's way of living, he also lost his prize, escaped death, and let down all of them consistently in his search for a greater Takenna Life. He wrapped his arms around his body as he lay on his resting bunk, staring out the window at the nima until sleep took him over.

Farming and Foraging

Scion awoke to a chill air in his cotoom, which only meant one thing. A changing cycle was on the approach, and foraging for food and picking crops to store through the cold days would now be in full swing. Easier to wake on a day like this when trying to move and keep warm, he quickly ate tarfe and headed out of his dorsa to stand in the Kaian. He had let down his gean, so today he was going to make up lost ground for that failure. Freedom for Scion meant his right and willingness to choose his destiny, and today he chose to stand and wait for orders on what the tribe needed to survive.

Gaitartuwain accompanied the farming leader, Jultaiwa, and the foraging leader, Tutawnai. These three were jointly combined to ensure the survival of the tribe and appointed workers within the areas of most need. Each day the delegation of tasks could shift depending on weather conditions and what supplies were running short. The last time Scion volunteered to assist, he ended up with Gaitartuwain in tool making which did not work out so well for any that were involved. Suspect of the last mishap, it was almost certain that no one would put Scion back in that labor market. In fact, that was the first and last time he had attempted to work with his tribe.

Jultaiwa stepped forward. "Our tribal members, thank you for coming to the Kaian today. May Takenna guide you." He bowed toward the tribe, neck lacings draping, and then he stood and continued,

"We have seen some trouble in our fields and are not yielding as much as we feel we should. I will only take four of you today to work on our crops. As we have enough tools for now, Gaitartuwain will take his usual two to be safe and continue working on tools and storage for the upcoming cold days as planned. With that, everyone else will go with Tutawnai to forage what we can in the absence of crop growth." Jultaiwa then pointed to his four recommended workers and everyone else, including Scion, turned to follow Tutawnai.

Most of the community walked out to the West, following their leader, over a few hills and to a large bush haven that bore fruits to eat. These foods were in abundance and were stored in the Kaian until needed. Some of the tribe used the fruits to add to their own creations, like Jiana's tarfe. Rare, though, that she had used the fruit knowing it could be needed during the cold days and she found it selfish to gain for her own gean while others may starve. Others were able to use the sticks and leaves to make lovely things to wear or fashion into tools at Gaitartuwain's work dorsa.

Scion wandered further into the brush while most of the tribe scoured the outskirts. There was plenty of small fruits to pick off toward the front, but they were not the only hungry individuals that dwelled in Prima Dair. He slinked his way around and through each bush, looking for the largest fruits he could. Each worker was granted one fruit to take for their own, and the rest was stored for safe keeping. For that reason, he wanted the biggest item he could find to bring back to Jiana and Midawal to make up for his shortcomings the day before, and he found it. Scion took note of the seemingly insignificant plants sticking up out of the ground with their rounded tops, noting that in the oreon they were bland in colors of beige and off-green. He huffed a small laugh, remebering how Caipri had marveled at their beauty in the light of nima. Scion shook himself out of his daydream and ducked his head to peer through the dense bushes and spotted a large, green and yellow object hanging down just a few paces from his location. Slowly he made his way over, ducking under brush and lifting hoof over overgrowth, maintaining eye contact with his prize as if it were going to sprout wings and fly off. He reached out and plucked the fruit, admiring it in his paws for a moment. He could not hold the fruit with only one paw and knew this would be the largest fruit brought back to the Kaian. With a grin of satisfaction on his face, he shoved into his tarp and continued to look around. The walk had paid off, and Scion gathered seven large fruits before his tarp became very heavy and he had to return.

Try as he might to walk stealthily back through the brush, it was more difficult with the weight on his shoulder and Scion consistently lost balance. Hooves were not meant to walk gracefully across overgrowth in brush. A strong branch caught hold of the tarp behind Scion and brought him crashing to the ground, knocking the breath out of his lungs and kicking up the dirt below him. A few heavy deep breaths and a shake of the head, Scion felt an ache all over his body from the fall and dirt went up his nostrils. He reached out is paws to push himself up when he caught something between his paw fingers. He plucked up the smooth object and examined it, head tilting from side to side and moving it in his paw fingers. This was nothing he had seen before, a bright and shiny twig that went in a circle like the oreon and a sparkling fruit on top. Scion bit at the "fruit" but it nearly cracked his teeth, too strong to be edible. He held it up and tilted the item from side to side once more, and it flickered like a lanarai in the oreon light. Fascinating discovery! He tucked the item deep into his tarp and continued to make his way clumsily back to the group as her emerged from the brush.

Tutawnai stood in the tall grass with his long staff, waiting for the tribal members to return with their haul for the day. He inspected the gatherings as each member filled up their tarp and waited for others to complete their tasks. None ever wandered alone for fear of danger, yet there was little to fear in their land. Scion approached with confidence of his exploits, prancing his hooves high and his chest puffed out. He walked up to Tutawnai and threw his heavy tarp on the ground, which led to a giant fruit rolling out of it. Members gazed upon the large fruit with wide eyes and a short gasp.

"Oh, I'm sorry. I'll pick those up in a minute." Scion overly animated his journey to sit down next to the tarp, knowing full well that his fellow tribe members were envious of the fruit he had plucked.

Whispers amongst each other started to stir about

the size of the fruit, and Tutawnai glared at Scion with morbid curiosity.

"Scion. Where in Takenna's name did you find such a large fruit?"

"That?" Scion pointed to a large fruit laying beside him. "That was easy. I climbed through the bushes a little further inward and found it nice and tucked away deep inside. Only one fruit per bush that bore it down. Can you believe that? Nice size, aren't they?"

Tutawnai approached and then held out his paw to inspect the food. Scion tossed one up to him, causing his leader to juggle it between open paw and the other holding his staff before catching his balance. Tutawnai rolled it in his paws, looked it over, and then held it to his large, aging ear.

"Scion, I must say this is a spectacular specimen. We will not store these just yet but share among the tribe tonight to test it. If everything goes well, we'll need you to lead us through the brush to your fruit-bearing bushes."

"Yeah, sure. I can do that." Scion remained incredibly proud during the entire exchange, waiting until the tribe could return back to the Kaian. He stretched his body out on the grass, looking to the sky above, and waited for the time to return to the Kaian. While most of the Dolgaian felt that Scion was rather useless, this would definitely earn himself and his gean some favor if everything went decent.

The last of the members arrived with their full tarps and the group headed back. One by one, Tutawnai inspected the fruit, allowing one fruit per member as promised and the rest went into storage. Scion was last due to the discovery he had made and chose the largest fruit as his own before returning to his dorsa.

Just wait until Jiana sees this!

❖ ❖ ❖

A few hours after Scion's fruitful return, a loud voice called out to the members of Prima Dair.

"Tribe! We have an announcement. Please enter the Kaian."

Everyone poured out of their dorsas to hear the news. Announcements were rarely made on such a large scale. In fact, the last one most members could recall was the announcement of Caipri's birth as Sesuna. They all looked round at each other, light chatter filled the air as rumor started to spread of the new fruit that Scion had found.

Gaitartuwain spoke. "Prima Dair has been blessed by Takenna to provide new sustenance to the tribe. During the forage today, Scion found a large fruit which we hope will prove to be a great savior during the cold days. Our crops have not grown as plentiful, but perhaps this will be enough to supplement the storage for all. We have made a bite for everyone and ask that you come forward to share in this new fruit."

Scion and his gean held back. He got to bring home his choice of fruit and made sure it was the largest. Jiana and Shawartia already cut it open and they all shared a light snack when he arrived at home. When cracked, the inside was a stark difference from its outer green appearance. Vibrant scents filled the air and the edible fruit inside was a deep magenta pink. To the delight of all, the fruit tasted as delicious as it appeared.

"Well, my palawal," said Shawartia, "it looks like you have helped the tribe after all."

"Thank you, Midawal. Takenna guides me."

Scion and his gean retreated to their dorsa as the tribe continued to marvel at the new fruit. Scion touched his forehead to his midawal's. "I am sorry."

They pulled back and Shawartia smiled at her palawal. "Sorry for what, Scion?"

He looked at her confused, tilting his head slightly as his eyes softened and his ears slinked backward. "Midawal, I disgraced you and Jia."

Jiana grabbed his shoulder from behind, causing him to look back at her. In an instant, they could feel the words being exchanged between them. Jiana then turned to Midawal and stated, "Let's get you to your resting bunk."

"That would be nice, Jiana." Shawartia took Jiana's arm as they walked back to her cotoom.

The slip of his midawal's memory was rather troubling to Scion. He could not sit still and decided to go for a walk to clear his mind.

◆ ◆ ◆

As the great reveal came to an end, Caipri sat at the edge of the Fountain. Her paws were clutched to her chest as she looked upon the stone structure of their Goddess. The tribe had dispersed, retreating to their dorsas, as she rested with her friend Olicai. He stood beside her valiantly, giving her his comfort by his mere presence. Caipri bowed her head and gave her thanks to Takenna for the bestowment of the fruit upon their tribe and granting the chance of survival. Olicai fluffed his white wings briefly as he watched her, then flapped his tail feathers down to the ground as he bobbed his head from side to side as he watched her.

"Takenna guides us." Scion stated as he approached the pair at the Fountain.

He had startled Caipri and she gasped, likewise with Olicai but he squawked his excitement.

"Scion! You scared me. I didn't know anyone else was here."

He approached and sat beside Caipri, tossed a wiggle bug at Olicai, and they looked up the Fountain together.

"Sesuna, what do you think her plan is for us?"

"Her plan?"

"Yes, her plan. If Takenna guides us, then she guides us through to the end. If that is so, then what do you think is her plan for us?"

Caipri looked down upon the water at the base of the Fountain as she pondered the question. "I think that none of us can truly know what she has in store for us. We must have faith that she guides us on the path meant for us to travel."

Scion smiled and stood from his perch. "Well, Sesuna, good nima to you and Olicai. I am extremely tired from my exploits today and must get some rest if I am going to continue to find fruit for our tribe."

His long stretch and over exaggeration made Caipri giggle as she responded, "Good nima, Scion."

Memories and Regrets

As was her ritual, Caipri gave her nightly song at the Fountain of Takenna. A quiver in her voice, trembling as she gave her praise and a tear filled her eye. Olicai could tell that her tone seemed filled with sorrow on this day, and when she finished, he nudged her gently and looked up at her. He bobbed his blue head from side to side, eyes blinking, waiting to be confided to.

"Oh, Olicai," Caipri giggled, brushed the tear away, and stroked his head. "I am alright, my friend. I promise."

The foragers were making their final approach for the day, and Caipri knew that meant Scion would reach the Kaian soon. She stood and walked to her dorsa with her companion following close behind. As Scion entered the Kaian, he watched Olicai's long tail feathers retreat behind the door.

As soon as Olicai cleared the door, Caipri was pressed on the inside of it, hoping that Scion did not see her. Yet, she was also hoping that he had seen her. Caipri's heart and mind were torn in separate directions, not knowing if she could even tell which way was up. Her breathing increased as her heart pace quickened.

Taltaira rounded the corner to see her palawal standing there and Olicai turned toward her. Midawal senses were heightened and could tell that there was uncertain tension surrounding her palawal.

"Best not to stand there when your padiwal returns. He may knock you over by accident."

Caipri was startled by the sudden statement, not

realizing her midawal was behind her. "Oh, yes of course." Caipri stuttered and began to fidget with her fur. "I just returned and hadn't stood there for very long at all."

The truth was that she had been standing there for several minutes, lost in her thoughts, and Olicai knew it. He shifted his head toward her with disappointment for her lie, and she looked down at him with defiance. Taltaira pretended to not notice the exchanging glances between them.

"Come help me set up for dinner. Your padiwal has been rather busy of late with the successful foraging efforts and he'll be famished. Olicai should wait in your cotoom as we prepare."

Caipri and Olicai looked at each other with confusion. Midawal only sent him away when she needed a talking to, and neither of them knew what could have gotten her in trouble this time. Caipri shifted her head in the direction of her cotoom, nevertheless, and Olicai strutted slowly as he looked at her with worry in his beady eyes. He made his way to the cotoom and his long, white tail feathers receded from sight.

Caipri then assisted Midawal with dinner preparation in silence. She was not about to inquire the reason to dismiss Olicai as it would lead to being chided like a young palawal. Then it happened, conversation that Caipri dreaded to have with her midawal.

"Scion has really made strides with the tribe these last few days." Taltaira's tone was that of a prying midawal digging for more information.

"Yes, he has. Takenna has finally guided him to a purpose among us." Caipri responded very matter-of-fact to avoid further conversation.

"I've noticed that you come back to the dorsa immediately after your nightly prayer."

"I do, so that I must maintain my gean duty."

Taltaira wasn't buying her palawal's excuse. "You are avoiding Scion."

"What would make you - "

Taltaira faced her palawal, one paw on the table and one on her haunch before continuing, "Why are you avoiding him?"

Caipri huffed slightly. "Midawal, I am not avoiding him."

"You may think that you can lie to Takenna, but you cannot lie to your midawal." She wagged a paw finger at Caipri and then turned to continue her dinner preparation.

Caipri bowed her head with mild embarrassment. She was indeed avoiding Scion, and all together trying to avoid the conversation. She understood that her midawal must have a point, a point that she did not want to discuss in front of Padiwal.

Caipri approached Midawal to start her confession.

"Yes, I am avoiding Scion. I am flattered by his affection and if circumstances were - different - I might relish in such notions. But I am a Sesuna and my place is with Takenna."

Taltaira scoffed and swiped a paw in Caipri's direction as she continued to make dinner. "Your final destination may be at the Eye of Takenna, but other than Olicai you have no friends. You should have someone else to talk to, you know, confide in. You have never had a life where you could play freely with other palawals in the Kaian and I am sure it has been lonely."

"I confide everything with Olicai. Believe me, if birds could talk you'd probably beg for him to be quiet."

Taltaira laughed. "Talking birds! Now that would be a sight!"

The pair laughed and set the table, then sat down and waited for Gaitartuwain.

"When I was a palawal, Sciotain was my confidant."

"Scion's padiwal?" Caipri took a seat at the table as she intently looked upon her midawal for a full story.

"Oh, yes. He was trouble, that one. He had all of these ideas and always wondering what was beyond Prima Dair. For a time, I thought one day I would be a part of his gean but he was just so wild and free. Eventually, I knew that my heart was here, with the Dolgaian. Around that time, your padiwal grew to be quite fetching and my eyes wandered elsewhere."

The two of them giggled and Caipri tapped her midawal's arm at the remark before Taltaira continued.

"Shawartia was also wild, and so full of Takenna's Life. She became the free spirit that Sciotain needed to settle down, and your padiwal was the devout Dolgaian that I desired. Those young days though, frolicking in the grass and taking in Takenna's blessings were some of my fondest memories. Eventually, we all grow older and assimilate to the tribe. Those times can be unsettling, but also a sign of commitment to those of our kin. Your path is much different than ours, as you are Sesuna, and unfortunately you have been bound to the Goddess of Life since your birth. You need more freedoms before you leave. Allow others to bring you life while you can and hold on to those memories as you commit to Takenna at the Eye."

◆ ◆ ◆

The foragers made their way to the storage within the Kaian to put their findings in for the day, continuing to build the supply for the cold days coming. Scion had watched Olicai's tail feathers slip behind the dorsa door of Caipri and her gean, and he stared at the dorsa for a while as the others filed in and completed their tasks. Sutalai, a young Dolgaian of Scion's age, smacked Scion in the back to get him to snap out of his trance.

"Come on, Scion," Sutalai said. "Let's finish up and quit daydreaming of the Sesuna."

Scion smirked and smacked Sutalai back. "Hey, don't talk to the Fruit Finder in that tone of voice. Takenna would not look well upon you for disparaging her unique palawal that saved the Dolgaian from… certain death!" Scion reached with his paw fingers, dramatically, into Sutalai's face and stared deep into the Dolgaian's milky-brown eyes.

Sutalai stared at Scion in his pose before responding,

monotone, "Are you done?"

Scion straightened himself, readjusted his tarp and responded, "Yes, I am done."

"Good. I wouldn't want Gaitartuwain to see you amorously looking in his palawal's direction when you should be working." Sutalai turned on his hooves and bumped into Gaitartuwain. Sutalai jumped back, startled, as Scion stood behind him.

"Put your findings into the storage and return to your dorsas."

"Yes, sir!" Scion and Sutalai responded in kind and went back to their finishing duties for the day.

Scion emptied his tarp, threw it over his shoulder, and waved to his kin as he made his way to his dorsa. As he passed by Caipri's dorsa he stared, turning his head as continued to walk passed it. He then realized that Gaitartuwain was staring at him from the other side of the Kaian, so he threw a salute motion to his elder as he pressed on to his dorsa.

Gaitartuwain assisted the tribe with the end of day duties before closing up his tool dorsa for the night. He shook his head as he continued to think about Scion's fondness for Caipri. So much of Sciotain lived on in the palawal, and the resemblance was striking. While Taltaira had originally fancied the freedom-loving Dolgaian, Gairtartuwain had won the heart of the one he loved. Old memories of his brethren running about in the Kaian played in his mind while he tidied his tools and made ready for the next oreon. He closed up his tool dorsa and crossed the Kaian to his gean dorsa, but before he entered he could hear Caipri and Taltaira talking inside. Then he heard laughter, followed by more talking that he could barely hear but then he heard Sciotain's name. Thinking about him, and hearing his name out loud, made Gaitartuwain hunch over with sadness and his ears laid back against his head. His friend, well sort of, was welcomed to Takenna much too soon. His disappearance left Shawartia alone to care for Jiana and Scion.

When Gaitartuwain felt the conversation hit a stopping point, he entered through the door. He followed his nightly routine, hanging his tack and knocking the dirt off of his hooves. He turned and walked to the table, providing a meager smile to his mate and palawal but said nothing.

"Hello, darling. You look weary this night."

Caipri moved uncomfortably in her chair. Padiwal had never looked like this before and she was unsure if she was the cause of his demeanor.

"It was a long day." Padiwal's tone was a sign not to pry. Caipri noted the tone for usage against her midawal for a later date.

The gean ate their fill, then Gaitartuwain stood and retreated to his cotoom in silence. He sat on his resting bunk with his head in his paws. Guilt sank into his mind thinking about Sciotain traveling to the Eye. None of the escort had returned from their journey, which moved to an adjustment in the leaders' selection of the escorts for the Chosen Palawals going forward. Caipri was not yet born, or even an inkling in his eye, when both he and Sciotain had apprenticed at the tool dorsa under the last leader. Taltaira

would have wanted for nothing as the midawal of a Chosen Palawal if Gaitartuwain never returned. Sciotain, though, already had Jiana and Scion was on the way. Pain twisted into his heart and he fought back a surge of tears as he laid down.
"It should have been me."

◆ ◆ ◆

Caipri and Taltaira cleaned up after dinner in silence, wondering what happened with Gaitartuwain. Finally, when their tasks were complete, Caipri grabbed her midawal's arm to inquire in a low whisper.
"What is wrong with Padiwal?"
Taltaira sighed and touched Caipri's paw on her arm, sadness fell on her eyes as her ears lowered. She knew that there was grief among the tribe for those that had not returned, but her mate felt most responsible for the padiwal that Jiana and Scion would never know.
"I fear that he may have heard us speaking of Sciotain. He bears remorse for not being chosen to escort the Sesuni on the last journey. No one could have known, though, that none would ever return. It wasn't fair to Shawartia, Jiana or Scion. The leaders made changes to the escort selections after that last journey to ensure that only young males and a gean member would escort the Chosen going forward."
Caipri then mirrored her midawal's expression. She

had never known the full story of Scion's padiwal and it pained her soul that some things could have been avoided. Now she hoped that her journey would bring the good fortune, as foretold, onto her tribe and spare those that dwell in Prima Dair.

Taltaira's hazel eyes attempted to appear happier than her soul felt on the inside when speaking to Caipri. "Don't worry, my palawal. Shawartia has a strong mind and fierce spirit. Others would have drowned in despair, leaving their young palawals to fend for themselves while wallowing in their grief. She made her way and her palawals have flourished under her guidance. Takenna's Life has a purpose, and She guides us all."

A Tribe Coming Together

As the bitter air came in, the entire tribe gave up on the crop fields that would not grow and sought out the new fruit from the Western rim. Gaitartuwain began making new tools to aide the others in chopping through the brush to make foraging faster and easier. Scion was appointed as a newly donned Foraging Scout and led the daily excursions into the bushes to seek new fruit. With collaboration, Gaitartuwain made a cutting tool with a long blade and handle for Scion to use to explore the bushes. After a few days of trial and another collaboration, a sash to go around Scion's haunches to hold the tool was made to free up his paws when needed to walk through the brush. With this tool, Scion had cut paths deeper into the bushes for easy access in and out. The success of this invention had begun the labor of creating more just like it so more tribal members could use it.

Brisk air circulated between the tree branches, bushed, and grass blades. Yellow and green leaves from the brush were falling to the ground as they shook loose from their base. Light and dark shades of pink leaves twisted in the air and came to a rest on the ground below, fluttering away from the trees whence they grew. Lush and tall grass was losing its height as the cold appeared to make the blades retreat within the warmer ground beneath them.

For weeks, day in and day out, the tribe had ventured to and from the brush with fruit. Instead of going once per day, they all made as many trips as they could in pairs to ensure they gathered as much as possible before it was too late. The main storage unit was almost full, and Gaitartuwain had completed building a new storage containment to hold extras. There was a general feeling amongst all in Prima Dair that this was going to be one of the worst cold days to date, and none wanted to be less than over prepared.

Those that were dedicated to their own craft or stayed back to help with young palawals all pitched in a helping paw when they could. Palawals were given the small task of helping to store fruit as they were brought in and gave a new tarp to members going back out to forage. Others were creating new tarps or cooking furiously to feed the workers and keep up their strength. With so much fruit, each member was rich in providing food to their gean at the end of the day.

Scion, too, had a tarp but he filled it at the end of the day when his scouting was no longer needed. As oreon crept slowly behind the grasslands, Scion used this opportunity to forage for himself before the long trek home. Tutawnai was Scion's partner on the journey back to the Kaian.

"Well, Tutawnai! Another exciting day with plentiful food to eat. We are nearing the end of time when we can still forage, and I just hope that they continue to sprout before we have to stop the adventure."

"Yes, Scion. I agree. The air is getting colder, and oreon light is getting shorter. I fear we may not have many more days left to forage and feed the Dolgaian."

They both walked in silence for a moment. Scion was taking it all in: the adventures close to home, discovering a delicious fruit, perhaps the best was having the admiration of his tribe for the first time ever. Tutawnai, on the other hand, was muddled in his thoughts and bore a look of melancholy in his eyes. Scion took notice of this look after a while and decided to inquire.

"Tutawnai, are you alright?" Scion asked the question with sincerity, ears backward in the inquiry and feeling empathetic for his elder.

Tutawnai stopped and clasped his paws around his staff. "Scion, listen. Listen to the sounds of Takenna's Life. The birds, the air, the Prima Dair life around you. Your whole life, we have thought very little of you with your running off and not helping as much as we thought you should. Takenna has a purpose for you, my young one. You have shown yourself to be a true member of the tribe." He placed his paw on Scion's shoulder and said, "Perhaps it is time for you to assimilate and take my place. I am getting too old and this has been the most exciting my life has been as a leader." Tutawnai laughed deeply as he spoke, keeping a paw resting on Scion.

"Tutawnai, I appreciate your confidence in me. I just, I don't know, I think that my place in Ocaia is being laid before me. There is so much more out there, I can feel it. I am proud to have served my tribe at a time of need and find a fruit that will carry us all on through the cold days. I'm afraid I must decline your offer." Scion's head drooped down in slight disappointment.

He had never felt that assimilating was meant for him, and his heart pulled him in another direction. Tutawnai nodded and smiled at Scion, then dropped his paw from Scion's shoulder at last. The two continued their travel back to the Kaian to drop off the last tarp of the day. Scion handed the tarp to a palawal to disperse into storage and Scion kept one fruit for himself. He noticed Caipri and Olicai were sitting at the Fountain of Takenna, much later than usual, and he walked over to them.

"Takenna guides you, Sesuna."

"Takenna guides you, Scion. You have been rather busy lately. Making yourself an integral part of the tribe was not something I thought would suit you."

Scion swiped a paw in her direction, "Ha! No way." Scion threw a wiggle bug at Olicai and continued, "I'm just helping out where I can, you know? Ensuring the survival of the tribe before I leave."

"Leave? Where will you go?"

"That is the question, isn't it? I will follow my heart and just start walking. Who knows where I'll go and what I'll see? That is the part I love most, the unknown."

Caipri's heart sank deep inside her. How she wished she could just go where her heart told her to, where the wind blew and in oreon light. Perhaps nima light would be best as she was easy to spot during the day. She looked up at Scion, noticing he had been staring at her with his head tilted and a sweet look on his face.

"Sesuna, you make the strangest faces when you're in

deep thought."

"I most certainly do not." Caipri protested. She was a Sesuna and there was no way she could look odd.

"Actually, you do. Your nose scrunches up and you frown. It's easy to see when you are thinking too hard."

Olicai squawked as if to laugh while Caipri touched her nose and above her large, blue eyes. "Well, if I am thinking too hard then it's your fault."

"Yeah, yeah. Everything is always Scion's fault. Which, you know what, is finally fine with me. For changes to come the tribe will sing my name as a savior, the member who saved the Dolgaian from the coldest of cold days remembered." He struck a heroic pose and waited for an applause, a cheer, anything. Caipri just stared at him. He slightly looked in her direction, holding his pose, to see Caipri's cheeks about to burst as she held in her laughter. He slumped the pose and she started crying in hard laughter.

"Oh, Takenna have mercy. Scion, that was hilarious to see." Caipri and Olicai were rolling around, she was holding her sides as he was flapping his wings and squawking loudly.

"Okay, yes, ha ha, very funny. Oh! I haven't spoken to you in a while. You know, as I've been busy as the Foraging Scout. I found something the first day that I found the fruit. If you'll wait, I'll go get it and show it to you. It's very small."

"That would be lovely, Scion."

Scion returned a short time later, holding his latest discovery from several weeks back. He had kept it tucked under his resting bunk for safe keeping and away from potential prying eyes in his home, like Jiana. He opened his paw to show the item to Caipri and her eyes immediately popped wide as she grabbed the item from him. She mimicked his initial movements, rotating it back and forth to see the glints of light flickering with her every turn.

"What is this?"

"I'm not sure. I found it after I discovered the new fruits and hid it away. I take it out most nights and think about who made it, where it came from, and what its purpose could be. There is also something on the inside of the oreon circle. I don't understand what it means."

Caipri tilted the item to look inside the oreon circle. Ancient writing to them, the meaning was not discernable but it appeared elegantly written. She shook her head as an acknowledgement that she also could not understand the meaning of what was inscribed. Caipri then handed it back to Scion.

"When will you leave?"

Scion stretched his arms as he spoke. "I don't know. I've made some progress with the tribe so I think I will stay as long as we are still foraging at a fast pace. Leaving during the cold days may not be a good idea, but I'll depart when my heart tells me it is time."

"Well, Takenna guides you, Scion. You have made a difference here in our preparation and we thank you for your work. I must return to my dorsa. Good nima, Scion."

"Good nima, Sesuna." He bowed, then watched her

walk to her dorsa with her white shadow bird before returning to his own.

◆ ◆ ◆

  Scion felt that he had finally made progress, both with Caipri as well as the tribe. It was refreshing to also have made an improvement with his gean, considering how badly he had messed up with the lost neck lacing and bartering their means for a selfish reason. As he laid down in his resting bunk, a smile stayed on his face with content of his recent contributions. Knowing that Caipri acknowledged his accomplishments was the greatest triumph for which he could have wished.
  Sleep consumed his mind in darkness, and when he opened his eyes again, he found himself on the Western banks of the Savidi Mor. The object he had seen moving in the water had disappeared and his fellow Dolgaian approached around him. Stunned faces glanced at each other and mumbles were exchanged. Whatever had been in the water was now gone. Scion turned his attention back to where they had been sitting and the other Dolgaian were planting themselves back down to continue eating.
  "That… odd." The smaller Dolgaian was speaking, and Scion was now able to pick up details of the conversation although his sight was still hazy.
  "…The Eye… a couple of days… may Takenna guide

you, Sesuni." The other male, more broad in stature, made his exclamation.

Then the Sesuni spoke as they broke tarfe. "My fellow... thank you for the support... may Takenna guide you all... to the Eye."

Scion shook his head, hoping to dislodge whatever was hindering his hearing and better make out the details of their conversation.

"Scio... come and sit. We are near... we make our... the Savidi Mor." The Sesuni made his statement as he swung his arm in the air toward the mountains, and they stood to pack up.

The troop gathered the tarps and blades and began to wade into the waters of the Savidi Mor. The troop held their belongings above their heads as they walked through, water climbed up their haunches and slowed their speed. The smaller Dolgaian appeared to have trouble keeping his head above water, sticking his nose as high as he could as he tread through the current. Scion held true, faith in his Goddess and the promise of returning to Prima Dair weighed heavily on his heart. Finally, the troop made their way onto the Eastern bank and had to stop to catch their breath.

The Sesuni approached Scion, grinning from ear to ear as he grasped his shoulder.

"Come! We are nearly there."

The End of a Gean

Only a few extra days were granted to the tribe to maintain the gathering efforts of the new fruit and storing it away for the cold days ahead. Then, sooner than expected, the chill air rained down in pellets and powder for several days. None were brave enough to venture outside to barter in the Kaian and the paths remained empty. All gean within their dorsas were constrained to utilizing their own small storage containments for food source during this time of solitude. The air temperature plummeted, and in the wake of such a dramatic drop it was clear that Shawartia had fallen ill.

Scion and Jiana tended to their midawal with extensive care, hoping the climate conditions would lift and they could seek additional help before it was too late. Shawartia found it more difficult to eat with each passing day and then she stopped being able to drink water. Jiana cried in her cotoom as quietly as possible so as to not disturb her midawal, and Scion resorted to looking at his oreon circle item when he was not at his midawal's resting bunk. While they dealt with the looming sickness and possibly losing Shawartia in their own way, the feelings deep inside were the same.

Conditions outside did not improve, and Shawartia called her palawals into her cotoom. Low tones and rasping in her voice, struggling without having a drip of water in more than a day, she wanted to speak one last time. Scion and Jiana rushed in as had been usual these last few days, hoping Midawal would regain strength, drink and eat as she should, and would recover. Jiana fell to her knees, hooves striking the ground below as she collapsed in anxiety, and she clasped her midawal's paws tightly.

"Palawals," she coughed as she spoke, "Takenna is calling for me. I must return to the Goddess of Life, for with my life, another will be born. I very much look forward to seeing your padiwal's golden eyes again." Shawartia opened her deep, brown eyes as wide as she could to see her palawals for the last time.

Jiana began to sob uncontrollably and her body began to shake. "No, Midawal. You are going to be fine and we are going to take care of you. Just one more day, we should be able to get help on the next oreon light. Please, just give us one more day to get help."

Scion placed a paw on Jiana's shoulder while she knelt beside Midawal and cried. He then knelt down beside his sister, took her paw, and then took Shawartia's paw. His demeanor was much more restrained, and he cried quietly as he said a silent prayer to Takenna. He looked upon his Midawal, then Jiana, and squeezed their paws gently.

"Jiana, would you guide us through a song to Takenna. Midawal needs guidance to her final destination and you know I cannot carry a tune."

Shawartia laughed, and coughed, at hearing her son's last joke during her time in Ocaia. Jiana snorted and wiped her tears away while she slightly laughed as well. She shook over her emotions as best as she could and then began a prayer song.

By oreon light, Takenna provides
By nima light, Takenna protects
In living days, Takenna guides
In ending days, Takenna Life reflects

As Jiana's final note rang, Shawartia took her last breath and joined with the Goddess of Life.

Scion and Jiana cried in each others arms for a long time, longer than Scion usually felt comfortable but it was relieving to have someone to share this anguish with. They finally pulled away from each other, looked at Midawal, and knew it was time to ceremoniously wrap her for the final descent. They gathered her resting bunk cloth and wrapped her within it, gently tucking it around her body. When they completed the task, Jiana and Scion retreated to their cotooms.

Jiana's cries echoed through her cotoom and out of the dorsa window. Her pain of the loss within the walls could be felt through the Kaian and wafting on the chilled air that filled the land. Low hums could be heard from the Dolgaian, a sign of notice that one of their own had passed on to meet the Goddess of Life. The song made Jiana cry harder, and longer, as memories of her midawal danced through her mind in grief.

Scion wrapped his arms around his body as he heard the outcries of his sister. He, too, was mourning, but more in silence as within his own resolve in order to process the loss. As the Dolgaian hums grew, sending support to his gean at this time, tears filled his eyes as he felt the love of their tribe behind them. Scion unwrapped himself, stood up and walked to Jiana's cotoom. Her wailing was growing louder as she huddled herself on her resting bunk. He sat next to her, placed a paw on her shoulder, and bowed his head as they grieved together.

◆ ◆ ◆

A few days after Shawartia's passing, the cold pellets had ceased and the Dolgaian were able to hold a tribal ceremony in the Kaian. As Sesuna, representative for Takenna's Life, Caipri felt it pertinent to be the ceremonial speaker and sending Shawartia's spirit to stay with Takenna. The entire tribe gathered for this moment, holding paws and crying quietly while reflecting on fond memories of the deceased.

"Shawartia began her life, they say, as a tribal troublemaker." The crowd giggled slightly, replaying those memories in their mind. "While she began without a clear direction, her creation of honey tarfe was revolutionary and led to more creations over time. Joining of the crops and adding another ingredient had never been tried before her, and now we cannot live without it. I remember her tarfe was so perfect, so delicious, I'm evening drooling in my mouth just thinking about it. We are lucky that she passed this gift and life blessing on into her daughter, Jiana. We are lucky that she blessed our tribe with her son, Scion, who has recently been appointed as the Foraging Scout and saved us all from possible starvation. She was truly a remarkable member of the tribe. May Takenna take her life into her heart and reunite with her love, Sciotain. Takenna guides us, and may we guide Shawartia to her final resting place with the Goddess of Life."

In unison, the tribe lifted their paws in the air, and for a moment Scion felt connected to his Midawal and, for the first time, his Padiwal as well. Shawartia's covered body began to shine brightly, and then suddenly dispersed into glowing dust that lifted into the air. Her essence had now become one with the Goddess of Life.

Jiana and Scion hugged tribal members that shared the grief with them as the ceremony concluded. Caipri gave them both her blessings, a meek smile to console them, and went back to her dorsa. After all was done, standing in the frigid air, Jiana and Scion began to walk back to their dorsa. Scion wrapped his paw around his sister, as best as he could around her husky build, and guided her back to their dorsa. As they entered and knocked off the white powder, Scion realized that Jiana had hard crystals under her eyes that matted her fur.

"Jia," he said as he walked over to her, "your fur is matted from your tears."

Jiana scratched at the hardened powder for a second and then slapped her paws by her side in frustration, which led to her crying more.

Scion hugged her tight as she let her emotions go,

and then backed up to help get the mats out from her fur. His eyes were empathetic to her, a sight she rarely saw from her brother. Once Scion was satisfied that he had done all he could, he grabbed her shoulders and looked deep into her eyes.

"Jia, we are going to be alright. Midawal prepared us to live our best Takenna Life and you hold her recipe close to your heart. Once the cold days retreat, we will be able to survive."

Jiana snuffed her cry and nodded, hugged Scion and then lazily retreated to her cotoom.

Scion took this moment to sit at the table and stare around the main living area of the dorsa. He was reliving the memories of running around, poking Midawal and running away. Jiana chasing him, and Midawal chasing her. His golden eyes began to fill with tears again as he gazed about his surroundings, succumbing to the notion that she was really gone.

"Takenna guides you, Midawal."

◆ ◆ ◆

The cold days were drawing to a close. Jiana and Scion had faced a troublesome passing of their midawal but had survived the grueling part of the changing. Birds were coming back, light chirping could be heard off in the distance, and the oreon light was growing longer. Soon, it would be time to start over and resume tribal life again.

There was no means to make tarfe, not until the crop had grown and was refined for use. Scion felt the pressure of returning to his station of Foraging Scout and was less excited than when he was originally gifted this position. Tutawnai also passed, along with others, during the cold days. Selecting a new foraging leader was going to be top of everyone's mind and Scion did not want to be elected. He played over the elders in his mind that had more experience, someone to delegate and lead effectively so he could retain his freedom of choice.

With the warming air, he took up his tool and sash to head back to the bearing bushes to see if they were close to producing fruits. He said farewell to Jiana and left the dorsa on a mission. As soon as he entered the Kaian, members rushed him to ask questions about the supply and if he could find a way to forage earlier. He bounced his vision from member to member, attempting to answer questions and then another would interrupt.

"When will we have more fruit?"

Scion replied, "I have to go and –"

"Do we have enough left over in the storage unit?"

"That is something you will need to ask –"

"Scion, please save us with your fruit bushes."

Scion was overwhelmed and sprinted away from Prima Dair as fast as his hooves could manage. Heading straight over the hills and to the bushes, and he did not stop running until he arrived. The remains of the bushes were still there, bare and broken from the harsh winds and frigid air that was still vacating the land.

Scion slowly walked to his fruit patches on arrival, regaining his breath after the long run, touching the twigs and peering into the brush. No leaves, no growth, no fruit. With a huff of breath, fearful to return to Prima Dair, he slumped down on the still partially cool ground. Grass was peeking out, birds were lightly flapping over head, and oreon felt warmer than past days. In the quiet surrounding, he lay silently and gathered his thoughts as he also caught his breath.

"So, Scion. What tool can I make for you now to help provide for the community?" Gaitartuwain startled Scion and he sat up quickly.

"Oh, sir, Gaitartuwain. I didn't hear you coming."

"Didn't hear me coming? Your ears were close to Ocaia and my hooves are massive." Gaitartuwain roared with laughter and plopped down, not in a graceful manner, next to Scion and they stared at the bare brush together. "Some Dolgaian you are to not be more aware of your surroundings."

Scion shook his head at his leader's quick jab of words. "There is no sign of change yet. No leaves, which means that fruit will grow later than we had hoped." Scion threw a twig in the general direction of the bushes as a form of slight protest.

"Hmph. Well, then I guess we look to work the fields for now and see what we can do while your bushes decide to catch up."

"Oh, no, you misunderstand. These aren't my bushes. No, I just happened to explore deeper and find something much bigger. These have been here for as long as I can remember."

"Scion, with the passing of Tutawnai during the cold days, we will need someone to take his place. You don't have to keep it for long, just long enough for myself and Jultaiwa to name a true replacement. We know this is not what you see as your fate, and while we do appreciate if you decide to assimilate and become the foraging leader in the tribe, it is not something we will force you to do. Takenna must have plans for you." They both sat silently for a moment when Gaitartuwain continued. "Your padiwal was truly inspiring. You know we worked together, and he had some really out there ideas. I mean out there! There were some days that he'd come in and I'd be so tired of his talking, but he had so many ideas on how to make things better. We lost a true leader that day. Your midawal too, very similar in many ways, always looking at the problem and finding a better solution. They were a perfect match, and we all were better for it."

"Thank you, Gaitartuwain." Scion bobbed his head up and down, trying to hold back tears and not look weak among his much older, and stronger, elder.

"Please, call me Gaitar. I mean, what were my midawal and padiwal thinking? My name is so long, no one wants to talk to me!" Gaitar slapped Scion's back, causing him to lose his breath for a moment. "Well, I have to get back to making tools. I'll inform the tribe that foraging is not ready to begin, and we'll start the fields and appointing a new foraging leader."

Scion continued to sit in silence for a moment, reflecting on Gaitar's memories of his midawal and padiwal. He wished he had been able to spend time with Padiwal, but he went to Takenna before he was born and never returned from the journey to the Eye of Takenna.

Reconciliation

With the frigid, brisk air slowly leaving Prima Dair, the Dolgaian began to busy themselves in usual tribal life. Crops were being planted, tools were being made, and harvesting Takenna's gifts started. Jiana's main trade was honey tarfe, and she needed honey to continue producing Shawartia's famous creations while the crops grew in the fields.

Jiana took up her tarp, which was a rarity as she didn't much need to forage and headed out of her cotoom to find Scion also leaving.

"Good oreon, Jia. I see it's that time of the cycle to complete your dirty work. Would you like some assistance and company?"

While Scion's tone seemed sincere, Jiana felt there had to be a mixed sarcasm in the offer. She frowned and tilted her head at him with bewilderment, light brown eyes scouring his face to uncover what mischief he was up to. Silence led Scion to speak and, hopefully, end the awkward standoff at the door.

"There are no fruits to forage at the brush, and I fear if I continue to help make tools that Gaitar may knock the color out of my fur." He nervously laughed as it was a joke, and yet he also felt it a very real possibility under the pressure of a heavy paw constantly smacking his back. "I am available to gather peppulas for the baicher nests."

Jiana's ears lowered and her face softened. Her brother was, indeed, being genuine in his offer to help her.

"Yes, Scion. It would be nice if you came to help me today."

Scion opened the door but held his paw out to guide Jiana out first. She shimmied through with her oversized haunches and Scion closed up behind them before asking, "Where to?"

Jiana chuckled and began walking South out of the Kaian. As busy as the tribe had become, Scion did not fight the crowd to keep up with his sister. Being the tallest female, and having a distinguishable scar on the back of her ear, made it easy for him to follow her from several paces behind.

Once they began to tread into an open field, Jiana stopped. The wind kissed her fur as she closed her eyes and took a deep breath. Tears began to fill her eyes as she looked over the grasslands and memories of Midawal played in her mind. The new changing became a bitter reminder of the one Dolgaian that knew and understood her, taught her everything she knows about tarfe, and the only friend she had in her Takenna Life.

Scion walked up beside her, noting the tears but did not look directly at her as he spoke.

"Well, where do we start?"

Jiana surveyed the landscape as she spoke. "Certain peppulas draw different flavors from the baicher when they harvest and place in the nest to make honey. Yellow peppulas are the sweetest but added with the fruitful taste of pink peppulas is what I need. Today, we search for yellow peppulas."

Scion quickly recalled the light purple trees with

yellow peppulas during his Eastern discovery walk and near death escape from the prior warm cycle, and his stomach turned. That wretched smell seemed to materialize with the simple phrase mentioned by his sister. The wince on his face gave Jiana pause.

"Something wrong, Scion?"

"No, not at all." He waved a paw in her direction, not wanting to discuss his explorations to the edge of Prima Dair. "Yellow peppulas, you got it!"

The pair began walking and looking for their quarry, careful not to trample on peppula patches under their hooves. Tiny, yellow peppulas had begun to bloom in small patches of dark green leaves and they were diligent to dig them out at the root before gently placing them inside the tarps. Scion was observing Jiana as they worked, noticing her facial emotions would go from joyful, to sadness and pain, then joyful again. Midawal had trained her through the cycles on this task and he could see in Jiana's eyes that she missed their midawal. If Scion left Prima Dair as he hoped, Jiana would be alone.

"So... Jia... uh, do you fancy any of the Dolgaian males?"

She shot him a sharp stare as her ears stood straight up. Jiana said nothing but her eyes said plenty.

"Dolgaian females?" Scion asked with a cheesy smile.

"Really, Scion? What in Takenna's name makes that any of your business?"

"It's doesn't, but, with Midawal gone and our gean ending I thought maybe it's time for us to start our new geans."

"You desire the Sesuna only so I'm not sure how you plan on making a new gean yourself."

"I'm a lost cause, you know this."

They giggled, although Jiana tried not to. Both were still plucking up peppula patches as they conversed.

"Seriously, Jia. Any Dolgaian strike your fancy?"

Jiana let out a long sigh and then stared forward, thinking. She turned and sat in the grass, stretching her long legs and looking at her hooves. Scion came and sat beside her.

"It's difficult, Scion. I'm much taller than the others and there are few Dolgaian my size. I'm out of place. I don't think a new gean, my gean, is meant for my Takenna Life."

"Oh, come on." Scion bumped his shoulder into her. "Don't think like that. You are now the reining honey tarfe maker. Midawal's recipe is in your blood, your brain, and your heart. No one else can do what you do."

Jiana smiled slightly and looked at Scion. "Promise you won't open your big mouth?" Scion smiled and nodded. "He's a little shorter than me, but I have had my eye on Maichin for a while. He comes for honey tarfe but I have a hard time speaking to him about anything else."

"Well then you need to find something else to discuss. I know you are standoffish, but surely you can open up to him enough to get a conversation going."

"Standoffish?"

"Boring. Tarfe driven. Obnoxious."

"You're my brother, of course you think that of me.

I think you can be selfish, reckless, and also obnoxious."
"I can be, but not with Caipri."
"What's your point?"
"My point is that I'm still myself with Caipri, but she makes me a better version of myself. She brings out my Takenna light, and I pay her my affection."
Sounds of birds chirping and grass swaying filled the air as they sat. Jiana stood and gathered her tarp, then held her paw out to Scion. He clasped her paw and she pulled him up to his hooves.
"We're done for today. Let's get back to re-sod the peppulas and construct the new baicher nest."

◆ ◆ ◆

Jiana and Scion leisurely walked through the Kaian back to their dorsa to complete their task for the day. The pair of them were talking and laughing as they passed the Dolgaian members going about and working to provide for their own geans.

Caipri and Olicai were sitting at the Fountain of Takenna and noticed Jiana and Scion walking, and talking, and oddly laughing together. Beady, black eyes looked up at Caipri while her ice-blue eyes focused on them until they retreated into the dorsa. Caipri then looked down at Olicai.

"That was odd."
Olicai made a deep noise in agreement.

"Come, Olicai. We should also return to our dorsa to see if Midawal needs assistance today."

Sesuna and shadow entered their dorsa to find Taltaira tidying up. It appeared more that she was keeping busy and had less than important matters to attend to.

"Hello, Midawal. Olicai and I saw the most peculiar thing, and you'll never believe it."

"Oh? What did you see?"

"Jiana and Scion were walking together, and getting along."

Taltaira stood straight up, ears reaching to the sky in amazement. "You saw what? That can't be possible."

Caipri laughed and replied, "I know! Olicai and I couldn't believe our own eyes. I have never seen the two of them getting along. Let alone laughing together."

"Well, Takenna works in mysterious ways," said Taltaira as she laughed.

Caipri and Taltaira sat at the table, and Olicai jumped into Caipri's lap.

"Do you suppose losing Shawartia has brought them closer?" Caipri restarted the conversation, perplexed as to how two siblings could suddenly get along after many cycles of animosity.

Taltaira took up Caipri's paw as she spoke. "I think that may have something to do with it. Both of them lost their padiwal at a young age, and now they have lost their midawal. All they have is each other and by some Takenna miracle they have reconciled old feelings to mend a new relationship."

They smiled at each other and Olicai laid his head down for a nap.

"What will you and Padiwal do when I travel to the Eye of Takenna?"

Taltaira smiled, but sadness filled her eyes. "We will reconcile that you are fulfilling a great destiny with our Goddess of Life. I could not be more proud of you, my palawal. We will miss you, but this dorsa will still need cleaning and your padiwal will need much feeding."

The pair of them giggled as Taltaira stood and went back to tidying their dorsa, and Caipri stroked her feathered friend as he rested.

Nima graced the dark sky above and Caipri made another pass at the Fountain of Takenna after Olicai fell asleep in her cotoom. She gazed upon the stone Goddess, glistening in the white light and caressing the stone curves of her hands and body. Reflected light from the pool of water below cast an uplight back onto the statue and highlighted her face. Mountains, grasslands, waters and air made up her entire being and recreated in stone to give the Dolgaian a face to the Goddess of their praise. Caipri couldn't help but wonder if Takenna truly looked the same as the stone figure in front of her. Caipri stroked her paw fingers in the waters of the pool, staring at the reflection of Takenna that was staring back at her.

Caipri sat on the ledge, crossing her hooves in front of her as she perched on the circular stone feature. Her posture was next to the Goddess, and she stared up at

Takenna as she thought about what to say.

"Takenna, I feel lost. I know that my place is supposed to be with you at the Eye, but I feel this pulling within me that wants to lead me a different way. I want to be free, like Scion and Sciotain. I want to be able to adventure into the wild and wander where it please me. Yet, I also want to fulfill my duty and bring my tribe good fortune and pride. A Chosen Palawal doesn't happen every cycle, so I am greatful for my status. How can I bring good fortune to the Dolgaian if I do not wish to journey to the Eye of Takenna? It's sacrilege."

Caipri saw a tiny, white peppula growing beside the fountain as she spoke. She stared at it, then plucked it and played with it in her paw fingers. The nima light made it shimmer as she turned the peppula from left to right, and Caipri was tilting her head as she moved it around.

"Your creations are truly remarkable, Takenna. All of them from the smallest of baicher, to the lanarai, the peppulas and the birds. What makes me so special? What earned me the right to be born this way?"

Caipri's ears twitched as she thought she heard something, and she began to search around in all directions. She clucthed the peppula to her chest as she snuffed her purple nose to smell danger, and her large ears were perked up straight. When she was confident that there was no danger and she must have been hearing things, she loosened her posture and exhaled deeply. Caipri looked down at the peppula in her paws and dropped it into the pool below, watching it spin and flow with the ripples. Her bushy, bluish-purple tail fell to the side the fountain and graceful laid there behind her.

"Takenna, please, how can I serve you and love Scion? How can I be made for a life of servitude but desire more? Perhaps I am not the only one who has felt this way, and I may not be the last. Seeing the structure beyond our borders leaves me conflicted with our Takenna Life. I know that you guide us, from the beginning to the end. If that is true, then Scion was meant to find the structure, and I was meant to see it as well?" Caipri looked up at the stone face above her, hoping for an answer to materialize but none came. She then began talking to the Fountain as if she were speaking to a confidant. "Maybe I am making too much of this and my path will be laid before me soon. I wish I could see my path as you see us in Ocaia. I dread the day that I have to tell Scion good-bye, and leave to make the journey to the Eye of Takenna. I do not let him know how I feel as it seems cruel to let him know. I do know that I will hold him in my heart forever, regardless of the distance. If it was my path to hold him, and let him go, then I must do it for the sake of my tribe."

Caipri got off the ledge and turned once more to pay her respects to the Goddess. She bowed gracefully, then stood and looked upon Takenna before retreating back to her dorsa.

Takenna Nima

Tarshai was named the new foraging leader, and the new changing was upon them. Warm air caressed the fur of the tribe and bustling activity had begun. Scion maintained the Foraging Scout position and assisted the community in cutting new paths to get deeper into the lush bushes. The fruit growth was slow moving, but the tribe maintained hope that eventually it would pick up as the changes continued. For now, they resorted to the smaller fruits on the outer rim of the growth to eat while meticulously setting the stage for harvesting bigger fruits. The fields were also not growing as quickly as previous cycles, causing the leaders to shift work demands as fit to accommodate the depleating food supply for the tribe.

The nima light came through the warm evening air, large and bright, shining in blue. The Takenna Nima had arrived and a celebration was to be held in the Kaian. This was the sign of Caipri's journey to the Eye of Takenna, new beginnings and prosperity for the tribe while it spelled out her certainty of solitude.

Calm resolve fell over Caipri as she watched the beginning of her end in Prima Dair. Her deep conversation the other night seemed to outline the true path for her to walk. Olicai approached and stood by her right side, staring up at his blue-companion and waiting to join the festivities. His eyes were generally small, but today they looked bigger with the enthusiasm rising in the Kaian. Caipri looked upon him and smiled, then patted his blue feathered head.

"Will you go with me to the Eye of Takenna?"

Olicai made a soft cackling sound and rubbed his head against her purple leg.

"I can't promise that it will be as exciting as it is here in Prima Dair, but I would love to have you by my side for the journey and to fulfill my duties to the Goddess of Life."

Olicai took that to mean it was time to go, so he ran to her cotoom door and waited for her to follow. She rolled her eyes and for once was his shadow on the way out of the dorsa.

As was tradition, the Sesuna was praised. She was gifted with food from the members, extravagant neck lacings, graced with everything that Takenna had provided to the tribe and in return given back to the palawal of Takenna. Songs rang out from all corners of the Kaian in unison and most of them were dancing in glorious celebration. This would last three days, as the Takenna Nima only arrives after three full changing cycles, and then Caipri would make the long journey to the temple. The Chosen Palawals were only to make the journey after reaching a certain age, and Caipri had been able to bypass the last one. She made her appearances, held paws and gave blessings or thanks to the members. A smile graced her face, but deep inside she was in mourning. It was difficult for her to accept the change to her own life more than it was to accept the changes in Prima Dair.

On the first night of celebration, when the Takenna Nima appeared, Scion remained inside his dorsa. He was conflicted in saying good-bye to the one he loved and losing her for the rest of his life. Singing echoed through his cotoom and shadows danced on the surrounding confines. Scion was trapped in his solace while he held on to the oreon circle and attempted to drown out the celebrations taking place in the Kaian.

On the second night, he had wandered outside of his dorsa during the oreon light to lay beside the banks of Mizon Creek. There, he took in the sights and sounds of life in the wild and suppressed his feelings of loneliness. As the day drew to a close, he knew he would have to face the event of Takenna Nima. He stayed in the Kaian for a while but stood against the side of his dorsa, clapping along with the songs of merriment around him so as to not draw attention to his morose disposition. He watched Caipri from afar, walking through the crowds of the Kaian and thanking them for their praise. With every smile she bestowed on the others, his heart felt a sting and it made his stomach turn. He knew it wouldn't be long before she was gone, and the look on her face told him that there was no salvaging her potential to stay in Prima Dair with him.

On the third night, Caipri's final night in Prima Dair, he gathered up the courage to say good-bye and intruded for a dance. Scion passed through the crowds, never taking his eyes off of the Sesuna, and wiggled his way through to get close to her. She was dancing with her fellow Dolgaian, twirling and holding paws with palawals in her sequencesed movements. He said nothing as he held out his paw to her, gave her a wink and a smiled.

"Scion, you grace me with your presence. I would be delighted to dance." She took his paw and away they went.

They danced the night away, passing between and around other members as they laughed, giggled, and twirled in full excitement. They would come together, hold paws and dance apart, and he twirled her around. This was the last time he would hear her laughter, and he was soaking up every moment of it while he could. No other Dolgaian attempted to dance with the Sesuna this night and the tribe watched the pair in their last moments together. It was clear among the elders that Scion and Caipri were meant for each other, but Takenna's plan was going to pull them apart. Such was the plan of the Goddess of Life.

Scion was taking her in with every moment. The glint of her blue fur in the nima light, the lighthearted smile across her slender face, and her laugh so full of Takenna's Life on her sleek face and purple nose. Caipri's large, blue eyes squinted with excitement as she looked at Scion during their dance. He was also remembering the older memories, like when he first met her in the Kaian. Palawals meeting for the first time, she was timid and shy but still graced the tribe knowing well that she was special. Caipri had never been curt or demeaning about her stature, rather she was always appreciative of those that sang her praise as a Chosen Palawal. She was always kind to her fellow Dolgaian, including Scion despite his many short comings among the tribe.

As the nima began to shrink in the distance, the tribe was slowly retreating to their gean dorsas. Scion and Caipri flopped down on the Fountain of Takenna to regain their breath as the songs had come to an abrupt end. Still laughing and poking fun at each other, they were finally able to catch their breath.

"Thank you, Scion. I have never danced that much in life. I am so tired." Caipri was still laughing and breathing heavily while looking at him, her eyes sparkling in the sky and the tips of her fur glowing in the light. She fought back the words weighing heavily on her heart knowing that Takenna Nima was her calling to leave Prima Dair.

"You did alright, for a Sesuna." Scion had to break up the emotional part of the evening and resorted to comical relief in an effort to distract him from the end scenario. "Who will be accompanying you on the journey?"

"My Padiwal cannot as he is a leader, so Midawal is going to take his place since I am the only palawal. Customary for a member of the gean to escort is of high importance, you know. They elected for Gortainin, Maichin, and Sutalai as the security perimeter. Olicai will also join me and stay at the Eye while I fulfill my duties to Takenna."

"Excellent choices," the response was almost too hard to get out. Scion could not understand why the leaders would not have elected him to escort the Sesuna. He was also concerned that Maichin, whom his sister fancied, would be gone for quite some time and her chances to speak with him had passed. "Hey, while you're on the journey do not forget to catch a glimpse of the Tricornia. They are said to wander the regions near Joto at night."

Caipri laughed abruptly and pushed Scion's arm. "Palawal tales, Scion."

He shrugged and winked as he responded, "Perhaps they are, but what if they are not just tales? Midawal said that Padiwal confirmed he had seen them, so anything is possible."

"Scion, you have been an amazing friend. I will never forget you." She laid a paw on top of his. He smiled in return.

"Sesuna, you better get your rest before the long journey. I hear it will take many days to travel to the Eye of Takenna." Scion stood up quickly, and awkwardly as his tail got caught between his legs as he stood.

Caipri nodded and Scion escorted the Sesuna to her gean dorsa. Before she retreated behind the door, Scion quickly stopped her.

"Wait, Caipri. I mean, Sesuna. I wanted to give you my parting gift as well. Please, take the oreon circle with you so that you never forget Prima Dair."

Scion gave the item to Caipri from his sash, and she looked upon it as the most wonderful gift she had ever received. She held it close to her heart as she spoke to him.

"Scion, I am honored to receive such a fine gift. I accept the oreon circle, so that I may always remember you." Caipri pushed her forehead against Scion's, and they embraced for a moment. Each felt a sense of calm and exhilaration at the same time. Caipri then pulled back and smiled at Scion before she walked into her dorsa, leaving Scion alone in the Kaian.

Olicai was already passed out on the resting bunk, feathers sprawling in all directions. Caipri giggled at the sight of her companion and tucked the oreon circle under her bunk for safe keeping. She gently moved Olicai's wings to allow space for her to lay down beside him, using her hoof to nudge his tail feathers out of the way.

As Caipri laid there, her mind was reeling with anticipation for the journey ahead. She would close her eyes and try to still her thoughts, but it was useless.

"Why can't I rest as soundly as you, my friend?"

◆ ◆ ◆

Scion crawled onto his resting bunk, exhausted from a night of celebration with Caipri and content with himself for making the decision to be with her as long as he could. The night consumed him, dreamscape took over his mind and sat him back in front of the Sesuni.

Scion looked around and then up to the mountain peaks to the East. They were so close to their destination and eagerness was visible on the faces of his fellow Dolgaian. They exchanged arm punches and readied themselves to press onward to the mountains.

"I am truly blessed to have you all with me on this journey. I cannot wait to arrive at the Eye of Takenna and fulfill my duties as the Sesuni of Prima Dair."

Scion stared at him as he spoke. This dream finally allowed him to hear the conversation, so he took in a deep breath and felt the stale air of the land around them. He turned his attention to the ground and saw that the grass was dull and brown. Scion scanned the area around them and noted that trees were withered, brown and possibly dying. His concentration was broken when his Sesuni began speaking again.

"I admire your resolve for coming on this journey with me. It must not be easy to leave your gean."

Without hesitation, Scion replied, "The pleasure is mine, Sesuni."

The dream hastened the troop's journey, walking over the dying grass and into the mountains while following blue-colored markers on the path. Speech became silent once more as they continued to climb through the mountain pass, but the sense of smell ached his nose and bits of sound reverberated within his ears. The images slowed as they approached a wide opening between the mountains to expose a large body of water in the middle of a valley.

They had arrived at the Eye of Takenna.

The Journey Begins

The morning after the three-day celebration was hard for Scion to swallow. He awoke to a feeling of sickness in his heart and a body that seemed to ache. He was slower today in rising from his resting bunk and walked into the living area to Jiana. She stood there, with a fruit tarfe in her paws meant just for him, wearing a similar face that reflected Scion's feelings. Jiana learned that Maichin was selected for the escort and her chance to show him affection, or simply have a conversation with him, had vanished until his return. Scion took the tarfe and they embraced in a brief hug. As they backed away from each other, Jiana managed a slight smile to try and encourage her brother to be strong. He took the offering and smiled lightly in return, suggesting the same to her.

Scion exited the dorsa to a myriad of onlookers as the troop was about ready to escort their Sesuna to her final destination. Taltaira stood quietly with her paws clasped together and Olicai by her side, and the security escort stood like stone as Caipri said goodbye to as many members as possible. Scion and Caipri met eyes through the crowd. He tipped his head in a slight bow in acknowledgement, and she gave a slight smile in return. Just then, Gaitar instructed the troop that it was time to release the Sesuna and they made their way to the South.

Scion turned and walked out of the Kaian to the West, collecting his thoughts as he peered in the direction of his work. His stomach was turning and his eyes were fighting to release tears. This was the last time he would see Caipri, but her duty was important to the continuous life in Ocaia and duty to the Goddess of Life. Lost in his thoughts and self pity, he hadn't noticed the appearance of Gaitar, Jultaiwa and Tarshai around him. He snapped out of his trance and looked at the leaders head on, standing proud with a paw on his cutting blade to wait for orders.

"Scion," Gaitar spoke with a solemn tone, "you were not chosen because you are a leader right now. You may not be one of us by assimilation, but you have been critical to our survival through the cold days. As long as you are willing to help the tribe, we ask you to stay here among us."

Jultaiwa and Tarshai nodded in unison, signifying the solidarity of choice and reason why he was not chosen to escort Caipri. The decision hit him hard, but in careful consideration and explanation, he knew their decision was correct. Scion nodded back at the leaders, showing the ability to accept the honor to serve the tribe and allow Sesuna to travel with impartial escorts. Gaitar, as the Sesuna's padiwal, should have accompanied her as well per the traditions. He was a leader, and so he, too, stayed behind.

Gaitar approached Scion and placed a paw on his shoulder.

Looking to the West, mind clear with resolve to serve the community, Scion took a deep breath and then spoke. "Let us discuss the work distribution for the day."

❖ ❖ ❖

Caipri's journey began by heading South toward Joto. The main path was the same as the trail for travel to market with their closest neighbor. With this being the first journey since the cold days, the path was difficult to see but markers alongside the correct path were created to assist in the journey to market as well as the Eye of Takenna. These markers were made by the Dolgaian, upright and straight with a peak on the top, and an attempt to dye the stone in bluish tones. They had fashioned various colors of purple peppulas and water to create the dye, then soaked the stones for several days after the molding was complete. Each marker was a slightly different shade depending on how the dye took to its base. On each marker, a symbol to indicate how far they had traveled, and how far they had left to continue their travel, both to market and to the Eye. The journey would be long, lasting many oreon and nima rises. They walked beyond a large clearing, where grass did not grow as tall, marking a half-way distance to their meeting point with the Pomoko. The empty space was used for the market shared by the two tribes.

The escorts were relatively circled around the Sesuna and her midawal as they walked. Maichin was beside Taltaira, smaller then the other two and his gait was gentle. He was a kind soul and lived his life bartering the trinkets of his midawal. Sutalai kept watch next to Caipri. He was the middle sized male, and Caipri made note that he was not his jeery self on this trip. His face was hardened and not full of life as she remembered it to be. Gortainin paced behind them all, tall and muscular in his stride. To most females in the tribe, he would be a steal away from other crying hearts but Caipri was unphased by his masculinity.

Oreon was beginning to retreat behind the land on the first day, meaning it was time to stop and make setup for the nima light. Caipri and Taltaira would be given a shelter to hide the Sesuna's color as she shined at night in these wide open lands and was easier to spot compared to her companions. The security escorts gave them cover and provided sustenance, and then began to speak amongst themselves in light tribal gossip until nima's full presence high in the sky.

Caipri and Olicai sneaked out of the cover for a moment to gaze on the shimmering light cast from the trees, peppulas and grassland. The nightly twinkling of life gave her a sense of calm and peace, admiration of such beauty that could be seen in the dark under the nima light. Caipri brushed her paw fingers over the grass as she walked by, taking in the color and texture of the foreign foliage. The grass was becoming more yellow and orange, and more odd shaped plants glowed under the light of the nima. More than anything she desired to see a Tricornia, if they were even real. They were said to never be seen in the oreon light, gracing the night with stark white skin, four thunderous legs and hair flowing in the air. Their long, slender heads were noted to have a horn on their forehead and two smaller horns protruding from their chins. Muscular legs and body, but delicate hooves that gracefully trotted through the grass. After a short while, waiting quietly and lying in the tall grasses, Caipri and Olicai finally feasted their eyes on a group of these elusive creatures. There was a heard of six Tricornia grazing, all white and glowing in the nima light beaming down on them.

"Olicai," Caipri said in a whisper, "there they are. They aren't just a palawal tale, after all. They are so... majestic."

Olicai replied with a squawk, startling the Tricornia and causing them to flee at a strong gallop in the opposite direction. Caipri turned her gaze slowly to Olicai as he tucked his head in his wing.

"Well that is just perfect, Olicai." She looked back in the direction where she had witnessed the mystical Tricornia and huffed. "At least I got to see them just once. Come, let's go back to rest before someone sees that we're missing."

Oreon kissed the horizon and the troop pressed on. The land was covered in flatlands for a while, then they wandered over rolling hills. Baicher in Prima Dair were yellow, but the further South they traveled Caipri noticed the buzzing insects were transitioning to a bright orange-red color. Trees to the West could be seen on the far horizon as they walked parallel to the tree line. What started as a line of pink trees shifted to red and orange, and now orange and yellow. The transition of color was almost seamless, blending together on the way. Peppulas were also morphing into variations that Caipri had never seen, not even like the immaculate bouquet Scion had last brought to her from his exploration before the cold days. The petals were looking larger and more vibrant with each passing over the hills. Butterflies graced the breeze with their shining orange and black wings, kissing peppulas for a quick sip before fluttering off again.

   The escorts were stoic and quiet, Joto was just over the next hill so they all pressed forward to meet their neighbors and continue with their second troop. Sutalai suddenly tripped and fell straight into the yellow-orange grass under-hoof.

   "Sutanai sensi!"

   Caipri turned around and ran over to her escort. "Sutalai, what happened?"

   "I'm sorry, Sesuna. I tripped."

   Caipri looked behind him and saw that there was a small hole in the ground behind him. She shook her head as she helped her escort stand up. "It's just a small hole. You should be alright. Can you walk?"

   Sutalai responded, "Yes, Sesuna. I can walk, let's proceed."

   Caipri looked back at the hole in the ground, which looked as if it were dug by a creature, and wondered what could have created it. She turned back around, unable to answer the question as they had a mission to attend to, and continued to follow Sutalai as they made their way over the next hill.

Upon arrival to the Joto marker, the leader and troop were prepared and waiting on the edge of the coveted trees. Behind them, the trees were extremely large in yellow and orange leaves as they were untouched by the same cold days seen by Prima Dair. Peppulas around were an astounding bright red and orange, large petals spewing up from the ground or tree limbs as if proud to be seen. There were birds in varying shape and size, all of the colors flying about matched their scenery, and each variation was complimentary to the region. The Joto themselves, like the trees behind them, were incredibly large. They had a massive head attached to a long neck that came down to a giant body and enormous feet. Their color was brown on their feet, fading upward on their body in oranges and yellows to match their environment. Upon their back, Caipri noted that they had something like a wing but it was singular, starting behind the head and flowing down to the tip of their tail. It was fascinating to look upon the wing, swaying beautifully in the breeze unlike the rest of their massive body. Their Chosen Palawal was, as expected, deep purple at his feet and bright blue on top of his body. The wing on his back was almost white in color with sheens of blue shining in the oreon light.

Caipri's troop stepped forward and nodded in polite gesture, then the Joto approached to greet their Northern neighbor.

"My name is Mitato, leader of the Pomoko. This is Katsuki, Sesuni of Joto. We have our escort as well, Saktika." Katsuki stepped forward from the others and bowed his long neck. The escort appeared to be the Sesuni's padiwal.

Caipri stepped forward. "Takenna guides you. We look forward to the journey with your Sesuni and escort. I am Caipri, Sesuna of Prima Dair. We welcome your company."

"May Takenna be with you, Sesuna." Mitato bowed his head, then turned his attention to the couple leaving and nodded slightly to them before he turned to walk back into the Joto trees. The leader faded into the trees and disappeared, their skin and color so like their environment that it was a seamless transition.

"Let us take our leave. I am interested to learn more of your land." Katsuki's voice was slow, and low. He presented himself as dignified and genuinely curious about their new travel partners.

"Your land is truly beautiful. The trees are much taller than the trees in Prima Dair."

"Prima Dair does not hold residents that are as large as the Pomoko." Katsuki responded with a smile and Caipri laughed.

"That is very true. We do have large birds, though. Not quite as large as you but fairly close in size." Caipri fidgeted with her paw fingers as she stared down at the bright, orange grass beneath her hooves. "Tell me more about Joto, the things inside the trees that cannot be seen from outside. I would very much like to learn more about you and your kind."

"We have many dwellers among the trees. The Cacicos live in the treetops, jumping between the limbs and sometimes causing mischief to our tribe. They have smaller ears than yours, and long, slender tails. Natiko are ground dwellers, mostly, but much smaller than the Pomoko and very fierce. They keep to themselves, but their sharp teeth and long claws tend to drive others away regardless. They are also unmatched in their temper."

"What do you suppose makes them temperamental?"

"No one has been brave enough to ask."

Katsuki's tone was matter of fact, which made Caipri burst with laughter as they continued to walk.

The troop took their trek Eastward toward the Eye of Takenna. As they followed the markers, Maichin and Sutalai walked at the front, Taltaira walked alongside Saktika, Caipri and Katsuki continued discussion of their two lands, and Gortainin headed up the rear. As the Chosen Palawals were in deep conversation of differences between their traditions, Caipri was also surveying the landscape to marvel in beauty that she would never be able to see again. The dark, lush and tall grass was thicker than the blades of Prima Dair. She would randomly pluck a blade and fidget with it while she was engaged in discussion with Katsuki, then drop it and pick up another one. The Sesuni began to notice this trend after several times and was curious as to why she would pull the grass to play with it.

"Why do you pick the grass only to discard it?" Katsuki's speech was low and slow, probably because of his massive size and long neck, Caipri thought.

"Oh, I don't know. I am just feeling the difference between this grass and that of where we come from. Our grass is lighter, and thinner with a different texture. I am sorry if it bothers you, I will stop."

"You are observing by feeling it in your paws?"

"Yes, I suppose I am."

Caipri had not realized she had been repeatedly plucking blades. It was more of a way to help pass the time, but she was subtlety documenting the differences of grass in her mind while maintaining a conversation at the same time. Her mind began to wander back to Prima Dair, thinking of her tribe and thinking of Scion. She desperately hoped that they would be alright and prayed to Takenna for their good fortune in her absence.

Uncertain Means

Dolgaian gathered in the Kaian to wait for working orders. Scion stood next to the three leaders as they stood in front of the fountain, looking at worried faces standing before them. The fields were not producing crops with lack of rain in Prima Dair, and the fruit bushes were slow to grow needed food for the tribe as a quick meal. With food becoming scarce, there was also less need for Gaitar to build tools. Jultaiwai stepped forward to address the tribe.

"Members of the tribe, thank you for gathering so early. As you all are aware, the fields are in dire need of rain and the fruit bushes are not growing as much as we need. Rationing of available food will begin today as we continue to monitor our growth and supply. There is no work to divvy out this day."

Anxious chatter started to rise from the crowd, and Scion's muscles began to tense with his own apprehension to do something about their current situation.

"Dolgaian, please. Hear me." Scion pushed pashed Jultaiwa as he began to address them all. "I will take whomever will accompany me to seek aid in our cause. We cannot make the sky weep, but we may be able to find something to get us by."

The tribe, as well as the leaders, looked around at each other in curiousity. Proposing something new was not a widely accepted notion. Scion could see the slight terror on the faces of his kind, unwilling to go outside of the norm to provide for themselves and their families. Suddenly, Scion felt a paw on his shoulder and saw Gaitar standing beside him.

"I will go with Scion and we will take any of those that are brave enough to seek new ways of providing for the tribe. If we should find anything of value, perhaps that will spark our ability to build new tools and continue to grow our fields." Gaitar paused to allow the chatter to subside, then he continued. "We leave as soon as I have readied some tack and blades."

Gaitar turned and strode his large hooves passed the members, and Scion took a sigh of relief that someone would side with him. This could be the only savior for them all right now, but more importantly Scion desired to stretch his legs outside of Prima Dair if he could. Jultaiwa and Tarshai raised their arms in the air to signify that the meeting was adjourned, and the crowd dispersed.

Scion watched as his kin walked away with drooped ears and hunched shoulders. This was a sight he had never seen in his tribe before and the mood was rather grim. He tilted his head from side to side, then rolled his shoulders before pressing on to Gaitar's tool dorsa to prepare for a new exploration. One paw held tightly to the cutting blade handing from the sash sitting on his haunches as his other arm sung quickly with haste. He entered the tool dorsa without knocking to see Gaitar staring at his worktable. The table was clear and Gaitar's paws were pressed on top with his weight bearing down. Scion closed the door slowly behind him as he approached his leader.

"Gaitar?"

"What are we looking for, Scion?"

Scion turned his head and took a deep breath before he answered. "I do not know. What I do know and understand is that we cannot wait for Takenna to provide this time. We have to do something before the tribe starves."

Gaitar nodded then regained his stature, holding his large gait high and exposing his massive arm muscles. "Help me gather some tack and blades, and we will hope others will join us on this escapade."

The two of them gathered what the thought they needed and placed the necessities outside of the dorsa door. Once they felt prepared, they walked out to find three members waiting for their orders. Not as many as they had hoped for, but it was better than only the two of them. They all gathered what they could and then looked at Scion for direction.

"We will go to the North today. Perhaps there is more water available toward our neighbors in Josima Mora and we will see what is out there. We may not find anything, but we thank you for volunteering." Scion shifted his head toward the direction he indicated, then led the troop out of the Kaian.

Deep seeded feeling of fear for all Dolgaian was clearly noticeable by the lack of communication taking place on the adventure. Heavy hooves dragged behind Scion and he could hear the tension trembling on the ground. He kept his eyes ahead, seeking anything that could be of importance. Traveling too far outside of the Kaian was not done except for the journey to market with Joto or to the Eye of Takenna. Unfamiliarity was something the Dolgaian feared, but it was something that had to be done.

While searching the wide-open terrain, and unfamiliar himself, Scion beckoned his leader for some insight.

"Gaitar, do you know of anything to the North? Any beings or creatures, or water sources?"

"No, unfortunately. Creeks run through the lands but nothing more than that."

"Yes, and creek water will not be enough for what we need."

"The tribe does not wander outside of the known territory outside of the Kaian, Scion. Not like you and your –"

Scion stopped and turned to Gaitar, "my padiwal?"

Gaitar's eyes softened as he slapped Scion's back and kept walking forward. Scion did not often hear about Sciotain, his padiwal, not even from his own gean. Yet, this was the second time he had heard his leader bring him up since the cold days. Odd.

A large bird glided overhead and the Dolgaian dropped down into the tall grass to camouflage themselves. The light-brown beast with red leaved trees sprouting from its crown swooped over the land and landed far to the West of the path being taken. Gaitar stood and gave the signal that all was clear, and the troop carried on.

Oreon was passed its peak in the sky, and they had not found anything useful yet. Gaitar forced a stop to the exploit so they could graze on what little food they had. Tack and blades were set down as the members rested for a moment. Scion was not ready to sit and felt in his bones that something was tugging at him. He scanned the area, looking for anything to subdue the feeling that he was missing something important and worthwhile. As he was observing the landscape around him, he noticed a lanarai flittering in the air just a few steps away. A smile crossed his face as he walked forward.

"Hello. It's been a while, but I have missed your company."

The lanarai continued to float in the air and swayed from side to side as Scion maintained his approach.

"Scion?" The lanarai questioned in a high-pitched voice.

"Yes, it is me."

Scion was just about to meet his friend when the ground gave out beneath his hooves, ripping through the grass and under Ocaia's topside. He plummeted into a hole, not too far below ground but enough that when he landed his legs and hooves ached upon impact. Dirt fell on top of Scion as he coughed and heard calls from Gaitar coming from the hole above him.

"Scion?!"

"I'm alright. Try to find a way to get me out of the hole." Scion replied and continued to cough as he darted his eyesight around in the cave.

It was too dark, even for his large eyes. As he blinked the soil from his eye lashes, a small light appeared above his nose. The lanarai he had spoken to was hovering in front of him.

"Take a tumble?" The voice giggled as it spoke to

him.

Scion was no longer amused. "You could say that."

"Come. This way." The lanarai flew down a tunnel as Scion reluctantly stood to follow the glowing bug.

Scion followed the soft light coming from the lanarai as he traversed the tunnel. He was beginning to regret his friendship with the bugs as they had led him to discoveries and continues pain, both emotional and physical. His gait was lopsided, as the recent fall bruised his legs, and he braced himself against the walls with his paws as he walked.

After a few minutes, the tunnel suddenly opened into a large cave. The lanarai waited just beyond the opening as Scion stumbled into in dark room.

The lanarai spoke, "Come see."

Scion followed along the cavern walls, rounded and nearly flat on its edges. His paws glazed over the walls as he followed the glow bug, and he saw etchings made along the cave sides. The pictures did not make sense to him, things he had never seen before. When he approached the place where the lanarai had stopped, he gazed upon an image lit up by the bug. He touched over the sight, a being that looked that it was planting crops but something else that went into the ground and sprouted water from below. Scion's eyes widened as the answer was below them the entire time. He needed need to find a new source of water, just what was below the surface of Ocaia.

"Thank you, my friend." Scion stated to the lanarai, elated that he had found his answer to save the Dolgaian.

"Takenna provides."

Scion laughed and huffed deeply with his response. "Yes, Takenna provides. Maybe next time, please don't drop me from Ocaia into a hole without letting me know first?"

The lanarai giggled and buzzed back toward the cave entrance. Scion shook his head and followed his friend back through the tunnel. Hopefully Gaitar had found a way to get him out of the hole by now.

Gaitar and the three members in tow pulled Scion from the depths of the tunnel using tied tacks and sashes. With a good heave the retrieved him from the darkness of Ocaia's ground and they all rolled into the grass to catch their breath. As they all gasped for air, Scion studied the clouds above in the sky. A grin and boisterous laugh escaped him as he found relief in the sight of oreon light once more.

"Gaitar, I know how to save the crops."

The massive leader turned his head to reply, "What in Takenna's name are you talking about?"

"I saw a sign. I know a way to make the crops grow and it has been beneath our hooves the whole time." He turned his face to Gaitar, "We need to get back to the Kaian."

The troop was slow coming back to Prima Dair due to Scion's slow gait. They made do with gathering his tools and carrying them on his behalf while Scion walked to the best of his abilities. He had spouted his vision to them on the way back, explaining how he thinks that digging further into the Ocaia ground would provide the ample water they needed to grow the crops. It may not work at the fruit bushes, but some food was better than none.

Upon arrival, Jultaiwa and Tarshai greeted them to hear of their undertaking for the day. A full debrief was conducted between the leaders and Scion was sent back to his dorsa for the nima light.

◆ ◆ ◆

Dolgaian gathered in the Kaian to wait for working orders. Scion stood next to the three leaders as they stood in front of the fountain, looking at worried faces standing before them. Jultaiwa addressed them as he had done the day before.

"Our tribe. We have been blessed with a vision from Takenna. The venture made on last oreon rise was not in vein. We will need to focus our efforts on the fields today, so Gaitar will take four members with him in case we encounter his need, and the rest will come with me to tend to the fields. We are going to make some changes in the Ocaia ground to pull water from beneath our hooves."

With the daily orders given, most of the tribe followed the leaders to the fields. Once all were gathered, Scion stood before them to profess his vision.

"Dolgaian. We need to dig deep into Ocaia, like this, and between the crop lines. In these seams, we will space out our holes as we dig. Some holes will find water, and some may not. Gaitar and his members will be assisting with needed tools, but until then we dig what we can."

Blades were given out to all that were available, and Scion helped to place his kin as he remembered seeing the day before. He looked at his tribe, darting his sight all around, gathering his thoughts before he spoke.

"That looks right. Start digging, and if something breaks or if you have an idea to hurry our speed, then speak out immediately."

The tribe stabbed at the ground with blades and crop cutting tools, but it moved too slow to make progress easily. Scion watched vigorously as they struck away before he got an idea. He dashed to Gaitar's tool dorsa with an updated report.

"Gaitar! The tools are not working as well as we had hoped. They need something stronger, more edged or something, so we can cut through the ground."

Gaitar nodded but did not reply as he turned to his work. Scion could see the thoughts running through the leader's mind and took his leave. While he waited for progress, he went back to his dorsa to speak with Jiana. She was sitting at the table, unable to make tarfe as there were no crops to use for her recipe. Baicher were buzzing and had made a nice nest above the window outside, creating honey that couldn't be infused for food.

"Jia, how are you?"

She looked up from her chair and replied, "I am well. How goes the endeavor to save our tribe?"

Scion shrugged as he hung his tack. He gathered with

his sister, sitting next to her at the table. The silence between them was unusual as they generally threw smart retorts at each other. Scion took up her paw and they gently smiled at one another.

"We hope to make some progress today with the fields. You'll be able to make tarfe soon, I am sure of it."

Jiana sighed deeply, but said nothing. The gentle hum of the baicher outside was soothing to them both as they held paws. Scion looked out of the window, watching the baicher outside as they zigged and zagged between the peppulas and their nest. It was humbling to sit and take in Takenna's Life, even though he could not understand the dire situation they were currently living within.

Commotion began to come from the Kaian, and Scion let go of Jiana before jumping up to grab his task and sash. He turned to sister after he was ready, smiling at her but he did not receive even a glance as she wallowed in her own self-pity. Scion dashed out of the door and headed to the fields.

Gaitar quickly fashioned a new tool, one that was very sharp on two edges and a handle attached to the middle. The two edges would serve to cut into the ground, when one side was dull then the other could be used. He took his new tool out to the fields, found a spot that was deeper than the others, and hacked away at Ocaia. He swung several times, hammering his strength into each drive, and finally hit a soft spot. He swung once more, and water started to spill out gently along the ground. Dolgaian rejoiced and sang at the sight of new water as Gaitar stood proud before returning to his tool dorsa to make more tools. He tossed the tool to a member as he retreated back to his work.

Scion jumped with excitement and ran back to his dorsa to tell Jiana the good news.

"Jia! We did it, we found water beneath Ocaia!" She turned in his direction with a faint smile as Scion grabbed her paw. "You will be able to make tarfe soon, my sister."

"What about your bushes? We will forage fruit as well?"

"We may. The cycle is still young and I will do what I can. For now, we focus on what we can provide."

◆ ◆ ◆

After several days of digging dirt and rigging an irrigation system, the fields were beginning to sprout green plants. Scion and Gaitar focused their own time and efforts to assist the tribe in growing the fields first before turning their sights to the fruit bushes of the West. They did not know if the same methods could be taken, but it was worth a try.

Scion awoke with a dull ache caressing his body from the physical work he had been doing. He rolled his shoulders, picked his legs up one by one, then crouched and repeated these motions a few times before he was ready to work on his fruit bushes. Scion strolled into the main room to find that Jiana was not there. Curious as she always awoke before oreon kissed the grass of Prima Dair.

"Jia?" Scion called out for her, ears perked in the air to await her return response. She did not reply.

Scion checked her cotoom, but her resting bunk was empty and she was nowhere to be seen. She must have left early. With more pressing matters, he decided to go on and tend to his work.

He exited the dorsa to meet with Gaitar and Tarshai before they walked to the fruit bushes outside of the Kaian. The three leaders discussed probability of success in their new water retrieval methods as they approached the brush. Green leaves had sprung and smaller fruit was carrying on twigs along the outer rim, a better sight than last they had looked upon it. They said nothing, spreading out to begin work on digging for water around the bushes. Each of them hacked away at the dirt surrounding the bushes, driving their tools into Ocaia in hopes of creating more than one way to survive the cycle and prepare for the cold days.

As Scion swung his blade into the ground, he was focused on Caipri. He hoped that she was alright and safe on her long journey to the Eye of Takenna. He felt that she must be about halfway there by now, deep in his soul, he could feel her from the long distance apart. Sweat was building under his fur as he continued to dig, and then it happened. Water bubbled above the dirt and relief ran through Scion's veins as he called out.

"I've got water! How are you doing?"

Gaitar replied, "Not getting anything yet."

Tarshai echoed, "Same here, but I think I'm close."

"I'll start rigging my sight to see if I can route the water through the bushes."

Scion hurried to unload his tack with the tools Gaitar had made for this new sort of work. He pulled out the tools and started piecing them together into the ground. From there, the next attachment was moved to flow above ground and redirect water to fall above the intended areas. As he worked, he heard his fellow leaders call out their success as well and they began the same routine of assembling the tools toward the bushes.

Once they had completed their mission, the three Dolgaian gathered on the outskirts of the fruit bushes and watched the wind shake the leaves. Silence, embracing Takenna's Life. They all knew, without saying a word, that this endeavor was in her hands now.

While a productive day was a much-needed relief for Scion, he felt himself having trouble with his sleep once again. Perhaps thinking of Caipri so vigorously was his downfall to a restful nima this night.

Scion found himself in an open valley between mountains that kissed the clouds in the sky. The Eye of Takenna, he could feel it, the large body of water sitting in front of them was too beautiful to be anything other than the land of their Goddess of Life. The Sesuni shook paws with his troop and turned to him for the same gesture.

"We have arrived! My duties to Takenna shall now be fulfilled thanks to you all."

Scion shook his paw and gazed at the rock surrounding them. It was marvelous to witness the majesty of the mountains and the glistening, blue water of the lake. He took a deep inhale to admire the scents of the atmosphere around him, but the air was stale. He took a second look and saw that the trees were wilted, peppulas were not growing, and there was no sign of life in the canyon.

As Scion muddled through the sights, with lack of sound of sweet smells, the lake began to bubble. Black steam popped from the bubbles brewing atop the lake's surface and a grewsome beast formed. This monstrosity looked fierce, and before the troop could react that monster grabbed the Sesuni and struck at his fellow members. The moment went by in a blur, and Scion ran away. He ran back through the path they had taken, following the markers as fast as his hooves could take him. He darted around mountain sides, skirting dirt beneath his hooves and paws as he clamored out of the mountains. Open air and the Savidi Mor ran in front of him. He dove and swam across as fast as he could paddle, crossing the West bank and continuing to run.

Out of breath, he was hunched over and looked back over his shoulder to see a dark mist coming out of the same pass he had exited. There was no time to continue running, he must think of something to warn others of this monstrosity. As he heaved air into his lungs and attempted to process information quickly, he looked around for his best solution. He looked to the Southwest path and saw a marker, and it hit him. He ran toward the marker, picked up a rock and started carving his message as the shadows edged closer to him with each passing moment.

Danger. Eye. Monstrosity. Scio...tain.

The Darkness

When oreon fell and nima rose, the group stopped for rest. Caipri and Olicai took up lying next to Katsuki, as it was impossible to attempt to cover him at night, and Taltaira took the cover on her own.

Each day of their journey brought new sights and scents to Caipri's senses. She watched as the lands changed again from deep reds and oranges back to the subtle greens of general grass like her home of Prima Dair. The peppulas, vibrant and reaching for the oreon in the lands of Joto, were now smaller and lackluster. Although the new lands looked like the place of her origins, it did not smell or sound like Prima Dair.

After the first day of travel with their new companions, Caipri and her faithful bird rode atop Katsuki and Taltaira rode atop Saktika. The two pairs had a difficult time hearing each other speak the day prior and this made communication more effective. They continued to swap stories and spoke of tribal traditions. Caipri felt a great sense of relief in speaking with someone like her, someone that had similar feelings in being born different. Likewise, Taltaira found comfort in her travel companion as a fellow parent of a Chosen Palawal.

"The Takenna Nima celebrations were wonderful, and I was very happy to spend time with my tribe before embarking on the journey to the Eye. How do the Pomoko celebrate the Takenna Nima?" Caipri inquired as she and Katsuki.

"Pomoko have a sacred site in the depths of the trees

where we gather during special occasions." The Sesuni responded in his usual low, deep tone. "We gather at the Turnosan, it is our largest source of water. Pomoko gather around during the nima to sing our praises to the Goddess and bringing good fortune to our lands. The Chosen Palawal is a generous stature of Ocaia, blessed by Takenna herself to provide service in exchange for our tribe to continue to thrive."

Caipri patted Katsuki's back and replied, "Takenna provides."

On the edge of the tenth nima rise as a group, they set up to stop and rest. Once everyone was settled, Caipri and Katsuki chose a spot further away from the rest of the group so they could continue to talk. Katsuki was much too large to be seen as prey, likewise he was so large that he could be seen as a threat. This made Caipri and Olicai feel safe in their decision to be on their own for the evening. After many days of travel, the conversations between Caipri and Katsuki became more personal.

"Living among the Joto has been rather troublesome, so I am grateful to begin my journey to the Eye. Our lands are lush with tall, beautiful trees, but my shade is so different that I stand apart. My friend, Tutuli, she has always been my strongest supporter and stood up for me against the Pomoko." Katsuki's face soured as he continued. "I hope Tutuli finds happiness in my absence. We were practically inseparable."

"I am sure she will be alright. What do you mean stand against them? You are all from the same tribe. Are you not all of the same stature and respect amongst each other?" Caipri was solely focused on Katsuki's stories of Joto. She was intrigued with learning more about her Southern neighbor, more so than discussing her homeland of Prima Dair.

"She may, but she was so intent with my protection that we only had each other. I was not revered among my tribe, although I would be foretold as a bringer of good fortune when I made the journey. The other Pomoko were unkind to me because my color was different, and they kept me away from folly with them. I fear that her loyalty to me may cost her a plentiful Takenna Life."

"Takenna guides us, Katsuki. You needed someone to help you until it was time to make the journey, and the Goddess gave you Tutuli."

"Yes, perhaps you are correct. Did you have a Tutuli?"

Caipri giggled at Katsuki's question. His speech was different than that of the Dolgaian and she found it amusing as well as adorable. "I have a friend back home, but his name is Scion. He has always been a troublemaker and not very productive, but he found a new fruit before the cold days that saved many Dolgaian during the changing."

"Why would someone troublesome become the one to save others from trouble?"

"I'm not sure. He has a good heart, I suppose. His midawal had to raise him and his sister alone, and she was incredibly couragous. He's different but in a good way, always looking for adventures and finding new discoveries surrounding the lands of Prima Dair. He gave this to me before I left." Caipri showed Katsuki the oreon circle on her paw finger.

"What is it?"

"We aren't sure, but it is rather beautiful. In the oreon light, it sparkles in different directions. I've never seen anything like it. Have you seen anything like it before?"

Katsuki shook his large head. They sat in silence for a moment, both pondering the object and how it came to be in Ocaia. Caipri looked out in the other direction, away from Katsuki and Olicai, and noticed lanarai glimmering in the night for the first time since before the cold days. She stood up and then paused, remembering they were afraid of larger creatures.

"Wait here," Caipri directed.

They looked on as she walked slowly toward the lights. Katsuki tipped his head to the side wondering what she was up to, Olicai seemed to know better than to worry about her walking off as long as she was in his sight. Caipri continued to walk at a steady pace toward them, but with every few steps the lights were slowly retreating away from her. She had only met them once, but Scion had created a friendship with them and earned their trust, so she would have to earn it for herself as well.

"Hello, lanarai. I am Caipri, friend of Scion in Prima Dair, and Sesuna. I know I am quite far from there, but perhaps you have heard of him?"

The lights began to come closer to Caipri, causing Katsuki and Olicai to stir and try to stand. She held her paw out and looked in their direction, prompting them to stop, and nodded to reassure that she was safe. One lone light came close to her face, right above her purplish nose to emit a soft glow upon her beautiful, blue face.

"Sesuna," it said in a high-pitched voice. "Scion is a known friend from afar."

"Yes! Yes, I met some of you, well sort of, before the cold days. I was wondering if you all could be my friends too?"

"Friends?"

"Yes, friends. Someone to talk to, you know. The Eye of Takenna may get lonely and there is only so much that Olicai can say to me."

Caipri looked back at her bird while giggling, and then looked back at the lanarai bug which had gotten much closer to her blue eyes than before. She was startled, and yet enamored, by the little light shining in front of her eyes. They stood there in the night, silent and staring at one another. The lone lanarai then began to fly quickly from side to side before emitting a reply.

"We have shown Scion the light. Now, we must show you the darkness."

All of the lanarai wisped away in a flash. Caipri stood dumb founded. That was not exactly what she expected from this encounter. What does that mean? She walked back to Katsuki and Olicai and sat down.

"What was that all about?" Katsuki inquired.

Caipri looked up at him and replied, "They said they must show me the darkness."

❖ ❖ ❖

A new oreon, brighter and warmer than the day before, rose into the sky and the troop continued on their quest. Katsuki and Caipri were silent, deep in thought about the night before and what the lanarai's message meant. Olicai sat perched next to Caipri and wrapped in her lush, blue tail as he looked around in observance of the landscape with great content that he was not walking.

Now we must show you the darkness. Caipri was mulling over the encounter, attempting to decode the meaning of what was spoken to her.

No one else seemed to know about the 'something,' or possibly other 'somethings,' that were in Ocaia. Caipri had kept the oreon circle and the evening adventure with Scion to herself, with the exception of telling Katsuki about the object. Both of these new experiences were shown to her at night. Could that be what they meant?

Taltaira and Saktika noticed the solemn palawals and lack of conversation that they had seen take place over the last couple of days. The parents spoke quietly about it and then decided to do the parental thing: pry. Saktika made his way over with Taltaira upon his back.

"Hello, there!" Taltaira started the conversation and waved at them with an overly large smile on her face. Caipri found the faux smile rather disturbing, and also rather unwelcome at this moment.

"Hello, Midawal." Caipri forced a smile in return.

"You both are uncharacteristically quiet today. Did you stop having interesting things to discuss already?"

Katsuki interjected. "My fair Dolgaian. I do not feel so well this day. Caipri is simply allowing me rest of talking so we may continue to the Eye on schedule."

Caipri rolled her eyes. That was the worst kind of response to give a concerned midawal. Maternal instincts would kick in and send her into a tizzy. As if on queue, Taltaira began rattling off.

"Oh, Sesuni! Perhaps we should stop. Do you have tatula herbs in this land? That aids an upset stomach. Or is it your head? That means you need a drink on the spot before you collapse, and certainly we cannot carry you to the Eye. Gortainin, we should stop."

"Midawal, please. If Katsuki needed more rest, he would say so. It's alright, and if it isn't alright then the Sesuni will be sure to say so. Right, Katsuki?"

"Yes. I will be sure to inform the troop if I cannot continue." Katsuki winked to assure their parental pair that all was well.

Moderately satisfied that their Chosen Palawals were alright, at least for now, they split away and let the palawals be. Caipri was tense after the exchange, not really in the best of moods to tell her mother that she has been fraternizing with other species that are not supposed to speak about doom and darkness. Olicai glared harshly at Katsuki, knowing that Caipri was less than pleased with the chosen response.

"I don't believe that was the best explanation you could have come up with."

Katsuki turned his head around to look at Caipri. "I panicked."

The pair smirked at each other, which manifested into giggles, which made them laugh even harder as they continued to try and suppress the comedic moment. They had to pull themselves together as quickly as they could to maintain the "sick facade." Caipri began to scan the surrounding landscape and held Olicai in her lap as she stroked the feathers on his head. She could see the Savidi Mor approaching closer, its water cutting through the land, which gave her a sense of relief that the long journey was coming to an end in a matter of days. Then she saw the next marker, which was appeared to be missing its top.

"Katsuki, please let me down."

He halted and then dropped his giant, dark purple legs down as far as he could to the ground, allowing Caipri to climb from his back. She stumbled on her way down as she hurried to get closer to the marker. The rest of the troop stopped when they realized their Chosen Palawals were no longer following. Olicai jumped off of the giant, flapping his wings to brace the impact, and chased after Caipri while squawking loudly.

Taltaira looked confused. "Caipri, where in Takenna's name are you going?"

Disregarding her midawal's inquiry, she continued to run toward the marker. Upon arrival, she concluded it was definitely broken and missing the top peak, almost a clean break with a slight upward angle on one side. The broken pieces were scattered on the ground, in a general direction, leading away from the Savidi Mor. Caipri investigated the broken stones and then the marker itself. She walked and searched around the marker in its entirety, and she noticed additional etchings on the river-facing side. She squinted as she deciphered the writings, looking as though it was done with haste with lines not completed or not exactly straight. Olicai looked at Caipri, then the marker, repeatedly as if expecting the stone to come to life and snatch his companion.

Katsuki stepped closer to Caipri, curious with her curiosity. As he approached, Caipri's expression suddenly changed from inquisitive to seemingly frightened.

"Is something wrong, Caipri?"

She looked up into Katsuki's large, blue eyes. "It says 'danger, eye, monstrosity... Sciotain.'"

"What does that mean?" Katsuki inquired.

Caipri stood, staring at her midawal. "It's Scion's padiwal. It was written by Sciotain."

Taltaira gasped and began to cry. "He never returned from the journey. None of them returned. What do we do?" She was frantically looking around at the others for a solution.

Caipri turned back to the marker, knelt down while placing her paws and forehead on the object. She closed her eyes and quieted her mind as she thought about the intentions behind the message. *What happened to Sciotain? Is this the darkness? What monstrosity would dwell in Ocaia that led Sciotain to etch this warning?* Her troop of seven would not be enough if there was danger ahead, and she did not know the travel status of Chosen Palawals from other tribes. Then it hit her, an idea. She stood abruptly and sprinted away, back the way they had come, yelling as loud as she could.

"Lanarai! Lanarai! Lanarai!"

She got to the middle of open land, gasping for breath as Olicai came bounding behind her, and waited for the lighted bugs to answer her call. Her mind was frantic, hoping they would appear for her in the oreon light. A buzzing noise began at a low hum and started to grow louder. A large swarm of dark specks were headed her way and halted right in front her. Clustered together, the looked like a hovering dark cloud and not the gentle, glowing lights of the nima night.

"The darkness, I think I understand now. We need help. Please, we need to tell Scion and the others in Prima Dair. There is danger at the Eye and Sciotain left a dire warning of a monstrosity."

The swarm floated there in front of her, then spoke to her in unison. A voice that when united became much lower in tone than when she spoke to one the night before.

"We show Scion the light, we show you the darkness."

"Okay." Caipri wasn't sure how to decode the swarm, like she was unable to discern their ominous warning from the night prior. "So, uh, please show Scion the light to bring me out of the darkness?"

"We show Scion the light, we show you the darkness."

Caipri shook her head as she thought about what to say to the lanarai. "Danger at the Eye, monstrosity, and Sciotain left a message for Scion."

"We shall tell Scion of the message." Then the swarm sped off through the skies, North and West in the direction of Prima Dair. Olicai made a horrendous noise and hid behind Caipri as the sudden departure spooked him. The entire group looked at each other with concerned and confused faces, not knowing what just happened or what to do going forward. Taltaira was now in complete hysterics as Caipri and her companion walked back to the group.

"Sesuna, what is your will?" Maichin spoke up to get clarity for himself and the others.

"I have sent the lanarai to fetch Scion, and whomever else is willing to help." She turned her gaze to the Savidi Mor ahead, and could see the mountains in the distance that led to the Eye of Takenna. "We will rest here for a nima and oreon rise. Tomorrow, we'll continue. Hopefully that will be enough time to get help. Perhaps it is nothing, but we don't know what happened during the last journey."

"Our last Sesuni escort did not return, either. We thought, perhaps, they fell on ill times or to devout their time with the Chosen Palawal. There were no reasons to think of that made up for their absence." Saktika recalled their last troop, sadness crept into his eyes as a realization that something terrible may have happened to all who venture to the Eye. "The Pomoko did not know what happened, and to not fret over circumstance, we agreed to not inform the new

Chosen Palawal when the time came." Saktika looked upon Katsuki as he spoke, "I am sorry, my palawal. When you were born a Chosen, we vowed to keep the last journey a part of the past that was never spoken. Your midawal and I-"

"You what? Thought it best to shield me from the truth? To shield Ocaia tribes from the truth?" Katsuki inquired with a deep and angry tone to his padiwal and Caipri stepped between the.

"Please stop. My tribe was aware that the last troop did not return and it did not repair old wounds to talk, or not talk, about it. We are here now, faced with the same peril that could still be lerking at the Eye of Takenna. Instead of thinking of what was, we need to think about what is here today."

The troop looked around at one another, but said nothing for a moment. As Caipri was about to make another statement, Sutalai spoke up.

"Sesuna, we will follow you to whatever end." He stood proud, and Gortainin and Maichin mimicked his stance behind him.

Caipri nodded at the group. "We wait, and then we find what is out there."

The Light

"Another pretty successful forage day." Scion was juggling fruit as he walked alongside Tarshai, who was walking with the former leader's staff in his right paw.

"Indeed, Scion. You are quite the fruit finder, especially now that we have been able to find water."

"I'm sure anyone could do it. I'm either lucky or have a unique sense of fruitful direction."

"And sense of water discovery?"

"That was also a lucky epiphany."

Tarshai huffed at the response, feeling that the response was a farse but none, including him, was willing to pry further into exactly how Scion was so knowledgable or lucky in his exploits. The pair walked back together and laughed over Kaian gossip, then they emptied their tarps and retreated to their dorsas.

Scion walked into his dorsa, hanged his tarp and sash and knocked off the dirt from his hooves before entering the main room. Jiana was setting the table with her daily made tarfe as he took a seat at the table.

"Jia! The tarfe smells delicious, as always."

"Thank you Scion." Jiana's tone was low and matter of fact.

"What happened today that made you so sour? You have your baicher nests and tarfe everyday, and yet you sound meloncholy."

Jiana rolled her eyes as she completed her task of putting tarfe on the table and replied, "I did not have a horrible day, necessarily. I am just worried about you."

"About me?" Scion placed a paw on his chest as he responded. "I have made a name for myself here among the Dolgaian. Foraging Scout, ring a bell? Now I have found a way to bring water from the ground to aide the fields and brush to grow."

Jiana took a seat across from Scion as she spoke, grabbing tarfe and not looking him directly in the eye.

"You're anomalous way of integrating into the tribe may not be the same of assimilation, but you have made a name for yourself among the Dolgaian. I am speaking about your future."

Scion looked up from his tarfe in curiosity. "My future?"

"Yes, Scion. Your future, as in your future gean." Scion rolled his eyes as Jiana continued. "Now, I was thinking that Mianai would be a good match for you, given her spirited nature and her gean's good nature. If you have others in mind than I am open to discussion."

"Jia, I do not want Mianai. She is a lovely member but I am not interested in establishing a gean at this time."

"Scion, I know you don't want to hear this -"

"Caipri isn't coming back? I am aware, Jia." Scion threw his tarfe on the table in defiance and stared at Jiana, who did not return his gaze. "I am not a palwal anymore and I have done a great deal in a short amount of time. I want my freedom to make my own Takenna Life choices. My gean will be mine when I decide, and not with whom someone else decides. Midawal would have never overhooved in this way, and neither should you."

Jiana looked up at Scion, their gold eyes locking as she spoke. "You're right, the choices are yours to make. I just want to make sure that you are not alone and that we both grow into our own geans someday. I just want you to be happy."

"I'm happiest when I am alone." Scion turned and exited his dorsa when he had his fill of tarfe and Jiana's pestering and left to Mizon Creek. Nothing gave him more inner peace than this place, especially at night.

He left the Kaian, empty and silent as he made his way to the South to walk through the grasses of Prima Dair. Nima light was glistening on the foliage, glimmering as the wind kissed it in passing. Scion took in a deep breath as the breeze wafted by and opened his eyes to a colorful wave grazing across the plains. As he made his way to Mizon Creek, Scion scuffed over the rocks that were above the running waters of the creek, his hooves making a click-clack sound as he stepped over them. He stretched out and laid down by the creek in his favorite spot, grass laid down at an angle from the time he had spent rolling front to back in the space. The stream rolled over the rocks in a jagged pattern, tiered in several levels which created a different sound than the other areas of the creek. The constant pitter-patter of water hitting the rocks emitted a melodious rhythm that drained the woes out of Scion's heart and soul and replaced those feelings with clarity.

His thoughts were tracking between his work on the brush and his feelings of Caipri. Scion was conflicted between the duty he held within the tribe, and the love he had for the Sesuna. He could smell the sweet scent coming from the blue fur off her back, and hear the sound of her laughter. Thoughts reeled back to the Takenna Nima, her smile wide and full of purity. Eyes of bright blue looked into his, and he was too frightened to tell her again about his true feelings. The last moment, their foreheads touching before she went to her dorsa, was a treasured moment to him forever as it was the closest to having her that he would ever know. Now, he could only hope that Takenna would give her safe passage on the journey from which his padiwal never returned.

The sound of trickling water had become disturbed and disrupted his dreaming of Caipri. A low hum was noticeable under the rhythmic waterfall and was out of place for Scion's serene environment. He sat up and looked around, attempting to identify the new tones through the cover of night. His ears twitched as his head swiveled from side to side. A light glow from the Eastern horizon had begun to creep up, and as the hum became louder, the light grew bigger and brighter. Scion was frozen in place until he realized what he was witnessing, a large swarm of lanarai glowing in the night. He had never seen so many packed together in large formation, they generally flew by themselves or in smaller groups. The swarm halted on the Eastern side of Mizon creek, straight across from Scion.

The swarm spoke in unison, the tone low and deep, which he had never heard before from his evening friends. "Scion, we have shown you the light. We have shown Sesuna the darkness."

"The darkness? What are you talking about?"

"We were given a message. Sesuna, she requests your assistance. She is at the Savidi Mor, traveling to the Eye. A darkness. Danger. Sciotain left a message. We have shown you the light." The lanarai then dispersed abruptly, going outward in all space and direction at once.

Scion stood speechless, not certain which part of the message he needed to focus on first. Caipri. Darkness. Danger. My padiwal? He shook his head to snap himself out of his trance and then ran back toward Prima Dair. Clearly Caipri was alive and in potential danger, asking for help.

◆ ◆ ◆

Running as fast as his hooves and paws would allow, Scion raced through the Kaian to Gaitar's dorsa. He beat on the door frantically and calling for him to hurry. In between knocks and yelling, he was attempting to catch his breath after the long trot from Mizon Creek. When the door opened, Scion fell straight to the floor.

"Scion! Are you alright?"

"Caipri... is... in danger." Scion's breathing was still catching up.

"What do you mean? How would you know that?"

Scion was struggling to get up, between lack of breath and the added fall to the floor, his thoughts were jumbled and his emotions were all over the place.

"Gaitar, this is going to sound odd. I made friends with the lanarai, they live out in the land and look like small lights at night. I was just at Mizon Creek and they told me Caipri sent me a message. Something about a darkness, danger, and Sciotain left a message."

Gaitar was taken aback at the mention of Sciotain, Scion's padiwal. He had not returned, nor did any of the others, from the last journey to the Eye of Takenna.

"That doesn't make sense, Scion."

"Gaitar, please." Scion grabbed Gaitar's shoulders and stared at him as seriously as he could. "Please trust me. Caipri must be in danger. We have to go to the Eye, now."

The troublesome palawal may have not assimilated, but there was no doubt of the fear in his eyes. Caipri needed help, immediately. Gaitar searched Scion's eyes before he turned away, grabbed is tack and headed out the door. Scion hurriedly followed, closing the door behind him, as they went to the tool dorsa where Gaitar worked. They searched the dorsa for any sharp tools and made a pile of them outside of the dorsa door.

"Gaitar, we need more members to help us."

"I know. Keep gathering blades, anything that we can use. I will call for an announcement."

Scion nodded and continued to dig through the massive amounts of tools and other sorts of get-ups that were used for the tribe. Gaitar stood in the Kaian and called to the tribe.

"Dolgaian. Please gather in the Kaian for an announcement."

Members began to trickle out of their dorsas, slowly and lethargically after being aroused from their slumber. Gaitar waited as long as his patience would allow.

"We have received word that our Sesuna and her escorts are in danger. They need our help. Anyone willing to travel and protect our Sesuna, please step forward and take up a blade."

None moved forward, only a sway of side to side motions occurred while they chatted amongst each other about the request. A quiet protest was becoming louder as Gaitar stood before them. Then Scion exited the tool dorsa, picked up a blade, and stood next to Gaitar. A sweeping hush fell over the entire tribe in awe that someone, especially Scion, would prepare to leave and face peril in the unknown lands of Ocaia. Jiana gasped and she began to cry as she saw her little brother prepare to go into battle. As loved ones looked upon one another, a small gathering began to form. Padiwals hugged their mates and palawals good-bye, answering the call to defend their Sesuna. More of-age palawal males also took up the call as their midawals cried.

Jiana pushed her way through the crowd and wrapped her arms around Scion, burying her face in his shoulder as she cried. Scion hugged her with his free arm, holding a blade in the other.

"You can't do this Scion. I cannot lose you too. I'm so sorry for what I said earlier and - "

"Jia," he said as he pulled her back to look her in the eyes, "I must go. We have to save Caipri and the rest of the escort. Taltaira, Gortainin, Sutalai... Maichin. They need our help." Scion raised Jiana's face using his knuckles and locked eyes with her.

They touched foreheads as she continued to cry. She nodded and then backed up. Her paws intertwined and she clutched them to her chest, tears falling to the ground as her head was bowed, ears tucked backward with sorrow and grief.

Gaitar leaned down to Scion. "Any idea how to get there faster?"

Scion bowed his head slightly with thought, trying to think quickly how to navigate many oreon cycles worth of travel into a simple one or two days. The fastest way would be to cut across to the East, but he knew the land on the other side of Prima Dair was not well suited for their hooves and could actually hinder their progress. If they went that way, they would also not be guided by markers for direction which enhanced the risk to everyone who traveled.

The nima and night sky suddenly became shadowed. A couple of large objects appeared overhead and blocked out what little light was above the Kaian. They were growing closer, coming down on top of the tribe. Large birds, landing as gently as possible around the Dolgaian and filling up just about all of the empty space that was available with their massive bodies. Other birds were making their landing outside of the Kaian to avoid taking up all of the small space provided among the ground dwellers. Gasps and squeals emitted from the females and palawals while the males readied themselves with available blades. A dark grey beast was staring straight at Scion through the pale pink petals surrounding his large head, protruding from the intertwining trees growing on top of his crown.

"We are the Kaizankuri. We heard from the lanarai that you may need assistance with your travel to the Eye of Takenna. Our clan can carry you there, if you wish."

The entire tribe was speechless and staring. Midawals were clutching their palawals closely and backing up against the walls of the dorsas behind them. Long had they been terrified of these creatures, and none had ever known that they could communicate. Birds that could talk. Scion stepped forward and bowed toward the apparent leader.

"Lord of the sky, we would appreciate your assistance and your kindness. How many are you, and how many can you carry?"

"We have twenty available and ready to fly. Each can carry three or four of you, depending on size." The leader was looking specifically at Gaitar, who was one of the largest in the community.

Scion looked back at the tribal males, standing at the ready with their blades. A smirk crossed his face.

"Let's ride."

East Bound: Caipri

Caipri stretched her limbs in the early light and opened her eyes to see streams of orange and yellow clouds dancing overhead. Such a beautiful morning and yet the day ahead could spell disaster for the troop as they made their way to the mountains in the East. Anticipation for what lay ahead made it difficult for any of them to rest well. The troop gathered and ate, silently as none wanted to discuss the potential dangers that they might encounter going forward. Taltaira was exceptionally shaky this day, fidgeting with her fur and on the verge of hyperventilating. After the group finished breakfast, Caipri stood and addressed them with a directive.

"So, I figure that we continue on the marked path. We'll follow the markers toward the Eye of Takenna, keeping our eyes wide and minds sharp. I feel that this darkness is not what we may think, but we must all be prepared. Let us hope that the lanarai were successful in delivering the message to Scion and that help may be on the way to assist with our journey."

"Sesuna and her bird shall ride with me, and Taltaira will ride with my padiwal, as we have been. This will give us additional advantage of views to things afar once we arrive to the Eastern bank."

Caipri nodded in affirmation.

"I can't do this!" Taltaira started walking back the way they had come, hooves stomping in the dirt in sobbing protest. Saktika slammed his giant tail on the ground in front of her, causing a high pitched shrill to escape her mouth. The Dolgaian jumped as they felt the shudder along the ground beneath their hooves.

"Taltaira," Sutalai gently touched her shoulder to regain her confidence. "Your palawal needs you. Do not despair, please. We need your eyes on top of Saktika in case of danger."

She buried her face in her paws and wept loudly. Sutalai embraced her, allowing all of her emotions to come out so they could press forward. After a few minutes, Taltaira looked up at him and nodded. Caipri, Olicai and Gortainin mounted Katsuki, reluctantly Taltaira mounted Saktika along with Maichin and Sutalai.

"Midawal, together we are strong." Taltaira nodded, and then Caipri gave her next order. "We cross the Savidi Mor. If anything looks out of place, speak up."

Crossing the river was made easy while riding on the backs of the two Pomoko. Caipri and her troop sat high on their backs as Katsuki and Saktika walked through the water. Eyes of the Dolgaian roamed and scanned over the land to spot potential threats or anything out of the ordinary.

A piercing squawk and flapping wings erupted from Olicai as he leapt into Caipri's grasp. She held him tightly and then looked around frantically in the direction he was focused on. Squinting her glass blue eyes in the bright light, she saw nothing startling. Caipri continued to hold and stroke her companion as he squealed and shook, seemingly with fear.

Gortainin also peered in the general area that started

the commotion.

"Sesuna, I don't see anything."

Caipri nodded, then looked to her midawal in front of her. Maichin was battle ready atop Saktika, while Sutalai held onto a panicked Taltaira with one arm and held his blade with the other paw. Maichin's stance lowered and his head leaned forward to see something more clearly through the light gleaming on top of the water. Tension in his stance suddenly became visible to Caipri before hearing his call to arms.

"There is something moving in the water and headed this way!"

Gortainin jumped up and stood close to Caipri, blade firmly held in his grasp to defend his Sesuna. Olicai called out again and became restless, violently flapping his wings and squawking. Caipri turned her body to the North and finally saw something coming toward them.

What at first looked like grass and twigs in the water grew larger as they moved forward. Defined bodies were brown and rigid, like rocks, with algae and grass growing on top which camouflaged them against the banks. Round eyes of muddy water color bobbed above the current, and a long snout preceded the body. They also appeared to have a long tail, covered with growing grass and cutting through the water behind them. Caipri counted two for sure, growing a concern that there could be more out there and undetected.

Maichin began an exchange to attempt to save them

from battle and keep the creatures at bay.

"Halt! We are escorts for Takenna's Chosen Palawals. Do not anger the Goddess of Life. Let us pass in peace."

It was then Caipri noted there were definitely three creatures in the middle of the water now. They were equally spaced apart and relatively even with each other, stopping their approach when Maichin spoke to them and floating on top of the Savidi Mor.

"Palawals of Takenna," the middle one spoke and her giant mouth splashed water with every movement. "There is great evil dwelling in the mountains. Many have entered. Only one has returned, but they too perished in the shadows."

Caipri put Olicai down and stood to speak to the creatures before them.

"What dwells in the mountains?"

"Danger. A monstrosity, they say." The far left creature spoke, a male with a deeper tone.

"Who called it a monstrosity?" Caipri asked.

"One that looked like you. They escaped, running mad and yelling as he swam across Savidi Mor. A shadow followed and dragged him back to the mountain after he made the Western shores." The far right female spoke, her eyes blinking sideways at the end of each sentence.

Caipri and Taltaira looked at each other with fear and thinking the same thought. Sciotain escaped and was taken back to the mountain.

The middle female spoke once more, "The Chosen should not enter. The shadows are always watching."

"Thank you for the information," Saktika interjected.

"We have all lost someone close that traveled to the Eye of Takenna and we must continue our journey."

"The shadows are always watching. You have been warned." The three creatures spoke in unison and then disappeared beneath the water.

The troop looked around at each other with mixed emotions of confusion and anxiousness.

"Well that was ominous, to say the least." Gortainin broke the silence.

More on edge than before, they continued to move through the Savidi Mor. Once the troop got to the Eastern bank, the escorts climbed back down and assumed their scouting positions. The mountains were straight ahead, appearing to be closer than they truly were. The last days of travel were upon them, one day to get to the base of the mountains and at least another day to travel through them to the Eye. Silence fell among them as each felt on high alert and looking around for potential danger. There was a slight breeze, quiet and wafting to the South. Peppulas were in dull shades of brownish-orange, shriveled and small. The grass, too, was in low tones of green-yellow.

"There are no birds here," Maichin said.

Caipri replied, "Good observation. I was wondering why it seemed so quiet. There doesn't appear to be life here at all."

The troop continued to creep forward, scanning over the land and remaining vigilant. With every sound the group would turn and observe in unison, eyes and ears keen on identifying the source of the noise. They all moved methodically in a group, swiveling their heads in all directions as they followed the markers on their path. A light fog began to form as they made their way to the mountains, decreasing line of sight from the ground and making it difficult for Caipri to see them from her perch.

"Escorts! Mount up."

Katsuki and Saktika knelt down to allow safe passage to their backs for the escorts. Gortainin joined Caipri, and Maichin sat next to Taltaira. Caipri looked around, panic set in as she realized they were missing an escort.

"Where is Sutalai?"

Everyone started looking down to the ground, Katsuki and Saktika bowed down their heads into the fog to try and find him. No one was silent now, yelling Sutalai's name in an effort to save their friend. Olicai's shrieking calls pierced through the air to assist with the desperation he felt from the others. Everyone slowly ceased calling for Sutalai, except for Caipri. Tears streamed through her fur cheeks as she continued to call for him. Sorrow fell across their faces, feeling there was little hope that he was still out there and alive.

After a few minutes of her cries and screaming for Sutalai, Gortainin lightly touched Caipri's back as she continued to yell out through her sobs.

"Sesuna, we need to keep going. Sutalai would want that."

Through water filled eyes, she continued to weep heavily and gasped for air as she stared into Gortainin's light brown eyes. She had failed to keep them safe, but there was nothing more to be done. She gathered what little composure she could and nodded, then said a short prayer.

"Takenna, may you hold Sutalai in your embrace. He was brave and kind. Guide him to your light."

Katsuki and Saktika began walking as Caipri snuffed her cries and wiped the tears off her cheeks. Nerves were shaken but they pressed on and they all had a watchful eye on the fog hovering below. As quickly as the fog appeared, Sutalai disappeared without a trace. They felt safe, for now, high above the fog while riding on the Pomoko once again. After a few hours, the fog dissipated and the escorts jumped back down to survey the landscape. Both gave the all clear and together they embarked on the last part of their journey for the day. Somber emotion made for a tense and quiet travel until they came upon the edge of the mountains. They all moved, but in silence and slight glimpses to one another.

Caipri was certain of her original plan, despite the loss of Sutalai. She set her hooves deep into the rotted ground and set down Olicai before turning to her troop. "We set up here and rest. We will continue through the mountains on the next oreon as we cannot see as well in the dark. May Takenna be with us this night."

◆ ◆ ◆

The troop slept huddled within the confines of the Pomoko. Their necks and tails touched, wrapped in a circle to enclose their smaller compatriots. The hope was to shield them all from potential danger during the night, and the plan succeeded. As everyone awoke to the morning light peeking behind the mountain tops, the next challenge stood high above them to the East and the next part of their journey was about to be underway.

"Gortainin, Maichin. You all will go ahead on hoof. It will be easier for you to make sure our neighbors will be able to get through the pass and guide us in."

"My Sesuna," Gortainin replied, "I will go forward, but Maichin should cover the rear in case of danger from behind."

Maichin nodded, then looked at Caipri for her final orders.

"Very well." Caipri gave her blessing with a nod.

Maichin made his way behind Katsuki and held his position, staring out at the land behind them to ensure that nothing was coming. Gortainin proceeded through the mountain pass, marked by the stones of Prima Dair and into the shadows of the mountains as the rest of the troop followed behind.

The path was upwardly lined with twisted trees, not full of life like the elders had spoken of but rather they drooped at the top as if they had succumbed to sickness and the leaves withered away. Caipri noticed a wavering leaf dangling from a tree above their heads, and with a light touch of wind it disembarked from its branch and came fluttering down to the ground. She watched the lifeless leaf fall and come to a rest next to Katsuki's large foot.

The air felt stale upon their nostrils and their eyes felt dry with the absence of humidity. Dust collected on the eye lashes and the Dolgaian were constantly wiping their faces to rid themselves of the crusted residue. The Pomoko had visible dust around their eyes and Taltaira took notice.

"Saktika, Sesuni, please let me help your eyes."

They bent their heads down for an assist, first Katsuki who responded with a slight grin, then Saktika came in.

Gortainin continued to follow the markers and signaled the all clear around each turn. Caipri was second in line followed by Olicai, Katsuki, Taltaira, Saktika and Maichin guarded their backs. They traveled as quietly as possible, looking and listening for danger ahead and up in the mountains.

They walked for several hours and decided to stop and eat when they reached a small and flat clearing, large enough for the Pomoko to stretch out a bit but still nestled within the confines of large mountainous terrain. Taltaira was silently panicking, and fretting, through the entire journey as she was too afraid to scream and alert the unknown to their location, and also afraid to run and possibly disappear like Sutalai.

"Midawal, come and sit with me." Caipri motioned for her to place herself next to her.

Taltaira was shaking but she sat beside Caipri and smiled meekly in an effort to show that she was fine.

"We will be alright, Midawal. If there is something out there, Scion will be able to help us."

"Oh, Caipri! How do we even know that Scion got your message? How do we know that the rest of the Dolgaian will belive the story? Even if they do believe him, if the message gets to him at all, do you believe that our tribe would be brave enough to face this peril?"

Caipri took Taltaira's paws into her own and looked her straight in the face. "I can feel it, Midawal. Takenna guides us all. Scion is coming to help us and he will find a way through Takenna's guidance."

Maichin leaned down to interrupt. "The light is growing darker, but oreon looks to be in the sky."

Everyone went silent and looked around. It was indeed growing darker, but not so much in the sky as oreon graced them high above with whisps of clouds hovering in front. Shadows were coming closer from within the mountain sides.

"Padiwal, help me create a perimeter." Katsuki spoke in a low tone, nearly a whisper.

The troop backed into each other, the Pomoko used their size to shield the others as darkness crept closer. Taltaira and Caipri held paws, Maichin and Gortainin stood at the ready, and Olicai was looking around frantically in the middle of the troop.

"The shadows are moving in odd directions," Caipri observed and whispered to her escorts.

The shadows were shifting. As the troop moved, so did the shadows. It was as if they were being tracked and cornered within the open clearing.

Olicai began pecking at Caipri's hoof. She looked down at the bird, and when he had her full attention he looked up toward a mountain peak to show her something. She followed his line of sight and saw it too. Her eyes went wide with fear as the darkness engulfed them all.

East Bound: Scion

As oreon became visible over the Eastern horizon, the Kaizankuri began to descend to the ground below. Through the night they had cut through the air and needed to take a rest for their wings. Carrying the extra weight of the Dolgaian on their backs made flying more laborious and expelled more energy than anticipated. A sense of great urgency pulsed through Scion's veins. He had to get to Caipri before something terrible happened.

"We cannot rest for long," Scion stated bluntly.

"Patience. We must rest our wings for a moment. We will be ready to fly soon."

Gaitar pulled at Scion's arm. "Come, let us eat while the Lord of the Sky rests."

The Dolgaian found it difficult to tread the ground beneath their hooves. Each step was a struggle as the ground seemed to suck them in and hold them down. Scion had seen this land for himself during an exploration, and what he feared if they had cut across to head straight to the Eye of Takenna. Curses were being exclaimed by the members, working harder than normal to walk and get into a group so they could share a meal. Gaitar took notice of Scion's seeming knowledge of how to walk more smoothly through the ground below.

"Scion, you seemed to walk easier than the others on this ground. What's your secret?"

"I have seen this land before."

The entire group gasped, horrified at the notion that

Scion had been to such an awful place compared to Prima Dair. A group of wide, brown eyes stared at him with fear.

"I suppose now is a good time to confess. I have been exploring outside of Prima Dair. I have seen things, and found things, that no ancient writings mention. The lanarai showed me 'something' North and East of our home, large and not like anything we have ever built. I found an oreon circle in the fruit bushes, small and shining in the light. The hole I fell into, while we searched for a means of survival, led me through a tunnel with pictures of ancient script that depicted bringing water from Ocaia ground. I have seen this land before as well, but only from just outside of the Prima Dair borders. I fell into the ground and found it difficult to get out, but I managed."

"What else have you been up to, Scion?" Gaitar's eyes narrowed when asked this question.

"I showed Caipri the large 'something' one night, and I gave her the oreon circle as my parting gift for her journey to the Eye of Takenna."

Scion looked slightly over to Gaitar, making eye contact. Gaitar was unmoved, eating his tarfe and staring harshly at Scion. The other members felt awkward about the exchange and turned themselves into groups away from the two during their standoff.

"You put Caipri in danger."

"Gaitar, I'm sorry. I love her and I just wanted to share something with her, show her things that she does not get to see behind our walls. I mean, if you really think about, maybe I prepared her for the journey. Perhaps showing her things that no one knew existed opened her eyes to see potential danger." Scion smiled as he attempted to turn his love's padiwal to his side, but Gaitar stood and walked away with a scowl on his face.

Rest and mealtime was interrupted when the leader of the Kaizankuri stood, stretching his wings and elongating his long neck. His clan followed suit.

"Come. We are ready to continue."

◆ ◆ ◆

The Kaizankuri flew in formation behind their leader. Scion surveyed the vast wasteland below as the large shadows glided over the small mountains of moving ground below them. There was little in the way of life on the land, and nothing challenged them in the sky. This area seemed as destitute as he imagined the first time he laid eyes on it. Scion squinted as he saw something odd down below. Two rather sharp peaks down below were not moving in the wind, but rather the land was wafting around them. He made a mental note to come back and see this wasteland discovery, if he made it back alive from the Eye of Takenna, that is.

When the land became green again, oreon began to retreat and nima would soon appear. Another stop was inevitable and the Kaizankuri landed. This patch of land provided a source of water and large enough space for all of them to rest. Scion stayed with their new friends while the Dolgaian broke off into their own huddle.

"You do not follow your own?" The grey Kaizankuri leader inquired with Scion.

"I've never been much of a follower."

"You worry about your last meeting with the leader?"

Scion shot a sharp eye at the beast. "He's not the leader. He is a leader, one of three."

"Come. You may stay among us. My name is Kalra, by the way. We have not had much of a chance for name sharing."

"Thank you, Kalra. Lord of the Sky sounds much better, though." Scion and Kalra laughed at the jest as they gathered with the rest of the clan.

◆ ◆ ◆

Light broke through the sky and Gaitar was already wide awake and ready to tackle the last part of the journey. His mate and palawal weighed heavily on his mind and his paws itched to hold them again.

"Lord of the Sky. When we get to the mountains, how do you propose we go through the pass?"

"Pass?" Kalra seemed confused. "We will not go through the pass. We will fly you all into the Eye of Takenna."

"No. We must use the pass in case Caipri and Taltaira encountered trouble before reaching their destination."

"I agree." Scion interjected solidarity behind his elder. Gaitar had an excellent point, even if it meant going a little slower.

Kalra gave it some thought before he replied, "We cannot fly low through the mountain pass. I am not certain we would even fit through if we walked."

The three of them contemplated their options. With the large size of the Kaizankuri, they may not fit but if they encountered a foe then their size would be desirable in a fight. Scion snapped his paw fingers when he had an idea.

"Your talons. Do you think you could climb or hold on to the mountain sides above the pass?"

Kalra raised his foot, wiggled his talons and played the scenario over in his mind as he watched his talons dance. The clan had never been on a mountain before. He turned back to look at his clan, all of which were awaiting orders. A smaller, green and gold female stepped forward. She stood as tall as she could with pride, neck held high and she spanned her wings as wide as they could go.

"We can try. For the Chosen Palawals." Zephra, Kalra's mate, glistened in oreon light as she proudly stood before them all.

The Kaizankuri behind her followed suit, they were willing to help their neighbors and save the Sesuna of Prima Dair. Kalra nodded at his clan and then turned to Scion and Gaitar.

"We will fly low when we arrive at the Savidi Mor to

see if there is a trace of the escort. When we reach the mountains, we will climb if we can."

Riders took their places and the crew took off.

◆ ◆ ◆

Once the Savidi Mor was in sight, the Kaizankuri descended to glide over the land. Their riders remained vigilant and surveyed the grassland below while Kalra led his clan closer to the mountains. Nothing seemed out of place to Scion. Not yet.

The large beasts landed at the edge of the mountain pass and riders dismounted. The Dolgaian fanned out to check the perimeter as a safety precaution on the ground while the Kaizankuri focused their attention toward the mountain peaks. Scion stood beside Gaitar, both of them looking at the mountain pass opening and the marker placed just to the side.

Gaitar was not willing to waste more time and said to Kalra, "Try to climb and see if it's possible."

The large leader approached the mountains, evaluating the best tactic to climb on the side. He extended his front leg and latched his talons into the rock to test the durability under his foot. Then he bent down and jumped up onto the mountain face. Using his wings for balance, awkwardly shifting his weight while digging his sharp talons into the mountain, he was finally able to hold his position and then take a few steps walking sideways above the mountain pass.

Pale, pink petals fell from the trees above his brow as he swung his tail around to gain better balance.

A smirk crossed Scion's face. This is going to work.

Gaitar gave the order. "Let's keep going. The Kaizankuri will walk above us through the pass. Be alert and notify me if you see anything odd."

The Dolgaian pressed on, following the markers that were made by their elders many cycles before. The path was long and winding and Gaitar took the lead to scout ahead of the tribe. Scion's constant feeling of anxiety since the meeting with the Ianarai swarm was beginning to come to fruition and he felt himself growing tired.

After a while, he laid a paw on a marker to stop and rest for a moment and suddenly his environment changed. His travel comrades, the mountains and the marker were gone. Scion found himself in a crystal-like void, alone. He looked around in all directions but saw nothing other than an array of colors gently swaying through the air. Scion glanced around in utter confusion and thought maybe he had fallen asleep and this was simply a dream. He slapped his cheek, but the scenery around him remained the same.

"Hello, Scion." A soft and gentle voice caressed the void and echoed throughout.

Scion pulled out his blade, ready to be attacked. "Who's there?"

"I am Takenna, Goddess of Life."

"Show yourself! I have to-"

"Save Caipri." The voice interrupted and completed his sentence.

Scion's mouth gaped open and he was twisting around to see who was speaking to him. Still holding his blade at the ready, he started to wander slightly from his original spot but continued to observe his surroundings. Then he noticed little specks of light floating around, like the lanarai flying over the lands of Ocaia under nima light. The lights were coming together in front of him, not like the massive swarm he had seen a few nights ago, but rather they were forming in a defined shape. A bright light shined and Scion shielded his large eyes reluctantly, still worried that he was in danger. When the light dimmed, he quickly raised his blade and stared at the creature before him. A creature that much resembled the stone Goddess on the Fountain of Takenna.

The tall and slender being looked down at Scion. Her translucent hair flowed like the wind, her skin a pale blue and glowing like the peppulas under nima light. Her form was made of grasslands, mountains, and river water. At the base of her flowing form was water, but it did not move about into open space as it should without confines to retain it. The Goddess smiled at Scion as she looked upon his bewildered face.

"I have shown you the light."

Scion fell to his knees, dropped his blade and bowed his head.

"Goddess of Life. Forgive my ignorance."

"You are forgiven." She outstretched her long and slender hand to him. "Please. Stand."

Scion complied and took Takenna's hand. He thought it rude to deny his Goddess's gesture, however he also found it out-of-place to take her hand as well considering her stature. Her smile then dissipated and her face became grim.

"Scion, Ocaia is in danger. My oldest brother, Malithaia, left this realm and inserted himself at the Eye of Takenna. He grew jealous of my land and my children, my palawals as you call them. His anger and jealousy has twisted his being into darkness while in Ocaia. He has taken my children for his own. You must stop him."

"Me?! But, my Goddess, I am nobody. Can't you go down and - "

"No. You, Scion. You saw my light when others could not. The lanarai are my only form of communication on Ocaia and you heard my voice. You seek to know and understand Ocaia when others care not. You may not share my likeness in appearance, like Caipri, but you share my heart and love for my creation. When the need is dire, you have brought yourself to do what needs to be done to save those you love. You are my true Chosen Child."

"Goddess of Life, I am overwhelmed. Certainly there is someone else stronger, or more brave. Gaitar would be an excellent - "

"No!"

Takenna's voice was thunderous, her eyes lit up with fury, and gusts of wind swirled through the void. Scion tucked himself down and covered his head as the pressure of air was hard on his body and frigid cold. He had angered his Goddess, and he was not only cold and beaten by the wind but also terrified of her wrath. If she could create life, she could certainly snuff it out.

The blusterous wind ceased, but Scion remained in his position as he shivered and waited for the Goddess to end his life for cowardice. He felt a gentle and warm touch on his head and he flinched. When nothing happened, he slowly removed his paws from his head and gazed up at Takenna, eyes filled with worry that he disgraced his Goddess. Her face was solemn, sad, and patiently waiting for Scion to reconcile himself. Ears tucked back, he slowly stood to face Takenna but did not make eye contact with her again as he was ashamed for his behavior.

"Your dreams, of the journey to the Eye. I placed those memories into your dreams." Takenna bowed her head with remorse as she continued to speak with Scion now looking upon her. "Sciotain's memories went into your dreams. I needed you to see what your father, I mean padiwal, saw before he met his end. Those dreams are his recollection of the journey he made with the last Sesuni. He met the monstrosity, Malithia, and tried to warn others of what transpired."

"His... end?"

"Yes. I am sorry. Sciotain and the troop were among the first to meet the shadows looming over the Eye."

Scion's eyes swelled with tears as he shook his head in disbelief. The Dolgaian knew, as well as Scion himself, that his padiwal was never going to return. The cut to his heart felt deeper as he now saw that his padiwal's last moments were shared in his dreams as preparation for what lie ahead.

"Let me show you the truth." She lifted her hand to the air and back down, the void lost its color as she began to turn colors into pictures as she spoke. "Malithaia is the first father of your world. His children were primitive, animals wandering about the land. Some were plant eaters, like you, while others preyed on them with their sharp teeth and piercing claws. Their life was chaotic and ended abruptly when a large rock collided with the world.

"Then my next brother, Valennin, had his turn to create life. He made the world unbearable, cold, and his children ultimately succumbed to growing warmth in the land. Our father scrapped Valennin's plans, cutting it short, and allowed Jestulai his chance.

"Jestulai was largely successful during his reign of the world. His children were a mesh of animals and what he called 'humans.' These children were intellectual, capable of higher thinking and skills at building. The large structure you found, the gift you gave to Caipri, and the pictures you saw in the cave, these were made by humans. These beings were the greatest creation this far of our attempts to sustain the planet life. However, they became greedy with time and ended up destroying the world themselves.

"I created Ocaia, taking the lessons learned from my brothers before me and attempted to blend those worlds into something more grand and beautiful than before. What I have learned since then is that my attempt to separate the tribes has inevitably made you all weak in the face of worldwide danger."

Color went back to floating about the void, and Scion stood wide-eyed with a gaped jaw. His breath hastened as he grappled with the information presented to him. A deep, historic lesson that went far beyond any writings of his tribe and explained all that he had been grasping to achieve.

"Oh, Scion. I understand that you do not understand the severity of this matter. You are always running, always looking for something better. Ocaia is the greatest place and I created it out of love. A love that you share for Caipri. You must accept this task. Only you can save Caipri and the others. Only you can unify the tribes."

Scion's blood still felt cold, his fur shook as his skin beneath it shivered. He was reluctant to accept that there could not be another to take up the call for the Goddess of Life. He stilled his breathing and closed his eyes. He thought of Caipri and the times that he caught her sweet gaze upon him. He thought of Jiana and how angry she would be at the missed opportunity to save Ocaia. His midawal, Shawartia, who was no longer living to provide the guidance he was seeking. Then he thought of Sciotain, his padiwal. Sciotain never returned from the journey to the Eye, and now Scion knew the reason that the tribe had been asking for many cycles. He opened his eyes and looked upon Takenna's crystal blue eyes.

"I will save Caipri and Ocaia. What must I do?"

Takenna smiled and said, "Take up your blade."

Scion followed the directive, picking up his blade and presenting it to Takenna. She placed her hands on the sharpened stone with her eyes closed, and within seconds the blade was shining brightly between her fingers. Waves of color flew out and around her hands as she concentrated, and Scion had to shield his eyes once more as it became too bright for his eyes to bear. He held on tight to the handle, which started to ache his paw as the forces of light were creating tension and movement in Takenna's power.

The light dispersed, and Takenna removed her hands. Scion looked upon his blade with wonder. No longer was this a stone cutting blade, but it had grown longer, thinner, and shined with the color of his Goddess's realm.

"Your blade now contains a piece of my essence. The only way to stop Malithaia is with your sword."

"A sword?"

Takenna giggled. "Yes, we'll call it a sword. A long blade."

Scion swooshed it through the air to get a sense of its handling. He looked upon Takenna, one last time.

"Goddess of Life, I am ready to accept your task."

Takenna smiled graciously at her true Chosen Child. In the blink of his eyes, Scion awoke, laying down and Gaitar smacking his face. He shook his head and looked up at his leader while gasping for breath.

"Scion! What in Takenna's name happened? Are you alright?"

"Yes, yes. I am fine." Scion looked at the other members, who were staring wide-eyed at him as if he were

infected. The Kaizankuri were clutched to the mountain sides and
staring down in his direction with worry.

Gaitar continued, "You lit up like the oreon and dropped to the ground. What happened?"

Scion slowly stood up and wiped off the dirt from his fur. He picked up his sword, still shining in colorful light. Everyone gasped.

"Takenna guides me. I saw the Goddess of Life."

A Fallen Item

Gaitar paced back and forth, rubbing his paws through his fur and over his ears, trying to grasp the story Scion just spilled out. How could it be that he, the troublemaker, was chosen to lead and save Ocaia from this creature? Tension could be seen on the leader as his large muscles tense and flexed on his arms, between rubbing his head and placing his paws on his haunches to grasp the severity of the situation. Caipri and Taltaira's life depended on their help and Gaitar was finding it difficult to accept the will of Takenna at this moment.

"Gaitar. I asked the Goddess of Life to choose you and she refused. Takenna was adamant and I could not refuse her."

"I'm sure... but, Scion... this is serious."

"I love Caipri, the same way that I love the mysteries of Ocaia. That is why she chose me, and that is why I am going to save her. I will save Taltaira, too. I promise you."

"Excuse me," Kalra interrupted, "we need to press on. I am sure that it looks easy but hanging here is quite tiring and stressful on our talons."

Gaitar looked at the Dolgaian, then the Kaizankuri overhead, and then Scion with his colorful sword. He shook his head.

"Takenna guides us. Come, Scion. Let's keep moving to the Eye. Lead us through the passage."

Everyone nodded and Scion moved to the front of the line, sword drawn and eyes peeled for any danger up ahead. As they rounded the pathway, Scion was now in charge of giving the all clear. Gaitar followed closely behind, so near to Scion that he was nearly stepping on his hooves and bushy tail. The clan was above them and searching around the high tops while the Dolgaian continued below on the mountain path.

Scion could see a clearing around the next corner and signaled for Gaitar and three additional members to go forward with him to check the area. When his assistants arrived by his side, he held his paw up for a pause, sword clutched tightly in the other, then gave the sign to move forward. They fanned out in all directions and Scion walked to the middle while looking all around with their blades drawn. The spot was clear, and Gaitar joined Scion in the middle of the clearing, placing his paw on Scion's shoulder.

"They made it this far, which gives me hope."

"Indeed," Scion replied and nodded, his eyes darting from side to side to ensure they were the only creatures on the clearing. He looked upon a marker, which told them how close they were to the end of their journey. "We will stop to eat and rest. We are getting close to the Eye."

Everyone gathered in the center to eat. Some of the Kaizankuri took a nap after they ate, not being used to walking sideways and above flat ground was exhausting to them. As Scion finished his meal, he caught a glimpse of a light glow upon the dirt on the opposite side of the clearing. He stood, maintaining eye contact with the light so he didn't lose it. His hooves tread lightly and by now everyone was watching him cross the small patch of land with stealth and silence. When Scion neared the object, he realized what it was and leapt forward to snag it off the ground. It was the oreon circle he had given to Caipri.

"Gaitar!"

The elder leader came bounding over on all fours and stood up quickly by Scion's side.

"This is the oreon circle I told you about. The parting gift I gave to Caipri."

Gaitar's heart began to race as he took the item from Scion, holding it in his paw fingers and thinking of what terrible thing might have happened to his mate and palawal. A frown marred his face as awful scenarios went through his mind, then he started to scour the ground frantically. It was nearly impossible to tell where they could have gone now that their troop had marked it up under hoof and talon. Frustration was setting in while observing the trampled dirt and attempting to look for another sign that they were alive. Gaitar was swiping at the dirt around his tribe and the Kaizankuri, which was beginning to startle them all as they looked upon a crazed creature seeking answers. Scion approached gently and leaned in as he spoke.

"Gaitar, they made it this far." Scion had to try and reassure his elder before he went mad with grief. "We should keep moving toward the Eye of Takenna if we have any hope of saving them from Malithaia."

The massive and angry Gaitar unleashed a deep throated scream of anguish, his head raised to the sky, muscles in his arms clenched, and paws clasped in a fist. His large body collapsed and his knees hit the dirt below him. The sound reverberated throughout the mountains, causing small rocks to detach from their base and roll down to the hard ground. Once the emotions were let loose, Gaitar gasped for breath, paws on his thighs, and was huffing deeply. The tribe looked away out of respect, heads down and looks of dismay crossed their faces. A twinge of sadness sank into Scion's stomach and it felt knotted. Tears welled in his eyes as his ears shrank behind his head. Hope was dwindling and mounting despair could be felt among them all.

"Scion," Gaitar was still catching his breath and heaving intensely, "we have to find them. I cannot lose them both. Not like this. Not like Sciotain."

"We will find them. Takenna guides us. Truly, she guides us. Padiwal left the message for us to find someday, and we will be able to complete this task." Scion placed a paw on Gaitar's shoulder as he was hunched over and heaving. "I have seen and spoken to the Goddess of Life myself, Gaitar. Our quest to save Caipri, Taltaira, and even that obnoxious Olicai will not be in vain."

"I do miss that white-feathered bird." He slightly laughed, trying to regain his composure.

"Come, Gaitar. We will follow the markers to the Eye." Scion stretched his paw in the direction of the mountain pass toward their destination.

Gairtar stood gradually, tall and massive with resolve in his stance, and replied. "Yes. We must proceed. Lead the way, Scion."

Scion smiled slightly, his golden eyes fixed on Gaitar and feeling empathetic for him. He knew that this must be twice as hard on his elder as it wasn't just Caipri on his mind, he also had to save his mate. Gaitar would do anything to save his gean, and Scion would do anything for Caipri. Scion turned to his compatriots to speak.

"Come! We need to keep moving. The Sesuna was here so we can keep hope that she and the escort made it to the Eye of Takenna. Stay alert."

Scion took the lead and began to wander up the mountain path and Kalra led his clan to take their place back upon the mountain sides. They followed the path, marker after marker. Everyone was more on edge as they proceeded down the beaten path between the large mountains. Eyes darted, heads swiveled to and fro, searching in all directions as they walked. The Kaizankuri were moving in a more methodical manner above their heads on the mountain sides and attempting to be as silent as possible, which proved difficult under their claws digging into the rock beneath their feet. Tension could be felt between all members of the troop and fear lingered in the air as Scion led his army forward. Saving the others was the ultimate goal, and only Scion's sword could stop Malithaia now if Takenna's word held true.

"Look! A moving shadow!"

One voice called out and everyone froze where they stood. Scion scanned the ground around them and looked up toward the mountains to check on their winged friends. Kalra and his clan looked with vigilance above, and the Dolgaian were turning in place to find anything out of sorts. Scion saw nothing else moving.

"I see it moving over there!" Another voice called, a member pointing to the left of the path.

The group looked around but saw nothing. Fur on the backs of the Dolgaian were standing straight up, tufted in bunches on their shoulders and their tails bushier than normal. Scion's eyes shifted from one direction to another, surveying the tight pathway and attempting to devise a plan.

Scion directed his army, quietly but with strong intent. "Move in closer, backs together. Slowly."

The Dolgaian followed his order and backed their tails behind each other, facing outward to look for danger. Scion and Gaitar stood next to one another but neither spoke as they kept their eyes fixated forward. With the tribe back-to-back, they had a full circle view around them on the ground. The Kaizankuri made their way downward a little bit, still hovering overhead but able to better see their friends below in case there was danger. Nothing else seemed to move as the group gathered into place.

Gaitar whispered in Scion's ear. "We should hold this formation as we proceed."

Scion nodded in agreement and then gave the order in the same tone as his last.

"We move forward in this formation. Blades ready. If you see something, anything, call it out. We do not know what may be out there. Stay as close as possible to the member beside you."

Quietly they proceeded, large eyes and ears on high alert and ready to protect the tribe. The Kaizankuri could not help but make some noise with their talons crushing the rock beneath them as they walked and glided between the mountain sides. Each crunch of mountain would cause the members to jump slightly as they held formation in the circle.

Up ahead, Scion caught sight of the next marker. As they got closer, Scion could see that it was broken and he walked ahead of the tribe to inspect the stone. The entire top was knocked off, leaving the bottom half sticking out of the ground. Scion located the last half of the writing to determine their proximity, then looked at Gaitar.

"We have arrived at the Eye of Takenna."

The Eye of Takenna

The tribe made it through the mountain pass to an open area with a large lake at the center. The Kaizankuri glided down from their perches and joined the Dolgaian on the land below now that there was room for their massive bodies. Several members still faced the mountain pass to serve as lookouts, while the rest stared forward and awaited orders.

"The air feels... foul." Gaitar made his initial observation to Scion and Kalra as they stood further ahead of the army.

Scion nodded. "I agree. And the Eye, it is black. If it were made in Takenna's likeness, it should be blue like Caipri. Life of Takenna has been drained from this place, inside and on the outskirts of the mountains."

Kalra interjected his observation as well. "There is a dark mist lingering overhead."

Little light came through the mists above, making more in depth observations of the surrounding terrain difficult. The space itself looked open, but the air within gave a feeling of closeness and slight suffocation. The edge of the mountains surrounding the lake were noticeable for a few paces, but darkness eliminated the ability to see to much further around the lake. In an unknown land, one that was only spoken about by the elders, did not make for an easy approach forward. The stale air was hard on the nose as well, making it difficult for Scion to concentrate as he scrunched up his tiny black nose in defiance of the scent.

Scion spoke to his fellow leaders.

"We should split up into groups. One group for each side of the lake."

Gaitar signaled and everyone broke up. One group with him and Zephra, and the other with Scion and Kalra. The leaders nodded at each other once everyone was in position and moved with their teams in opposite directions.

The clan walked with their wings against their backs and necks extended high to seek potential threats. The tribe moved through the giants, weaving under their legs and surveying what they could through the dark-filled air. The Dolgaian held their blades, quivering with dread made the blades unsteady in their paws. Gaitar led his team to left, and Scion led his team to the right. Scion kept close to Kalra's front feet as they made their venture forward.

"Who dares to enter my dominion?"

A deep voice echoed through the canyon. Brooding and dark, assaulting to the ears and making them tremble. Scion had never heard anything so sinister in all of his days, and it made his fur stand up.

"This is not your domain," yelled Scion in response. "Ocaia belongs to Takenna, the Goddess of Life. You are an intruder on these lands."

"Takenna." The voice was loud and hissed her name with disapproval.

Gaitar took his turn to chime in. "There is no place for you in this land. Dispel, and return our escort immediately."

"Dispel, you say? This was my land long before my

sister. I am the First Father. I am the one, true ruler of these lands."

As the voice spoke, the water of the lake began to bubble and a dark shadow appeared on its surface. A black, clouded beast came into form in front of the army. Two, shorter legs in the front with sprawling talons reached out and slammed on top of the lake, and two legs behind that were muscular and strong. A sweeping, black shadow spine appeared down his back and to the tip of his tail, which swayed violently with no rhyme or reason. Then his eyes appeared out of the black shadows making up the face, large and red, glaring from side to side at the armies on each bank of the lake. His face was long and slender with a large snout, sharp teeth bearing above his lip, and black water dripping from his mouth. The creature was a morbid sight to see.

"Malithaia!" Scion walked forward as he called out to the beast, and the demon snapped his attention in Scion's direction. "This is no longer your land. Return our gean, now!"

The giant, shadow beast laughed deeply at the demand. In a cocky and matter-of-fact way, he responded to Scion with his superiority.

"You are truly pathetic. So tiny and... adorable. Takenna was a fool to bring a creature like you into being. My children were much more superior in every way. Strong. Fierce. Brutal and unwavering in their desire to survive. What will you do if I refuse you?" Malithia snickered with his retort.

The insults nipped at Scion's confidence slightly,

noting that this being was much larger than he anticipated him to be. Takenna was tall, but she had not presented herself in this kind of manner and he was not prepared to fight such a monster. Scion rolled his shoulders, readied his blade, and then stared back at Malithaia once more with solid resolve. He knew what needed to be done and he was ready to face the demon. At the same time, Malithaia lowered his large head toward Scion.

"Tell you what, puny creature. If the lot of you can defeat my children, I will let your friends go."

The dense fog at the far end of the lake, opposite the mountain pass, dispersed. Against the mountain rocks and bound in black shadow were the members of their escort, Caipri and Olicai, as well as the escorts and Chosen Palawals from other lands. They all appeared to be asleep, or possibly just unconscious, and suddenly the entire army gasped in unison at the sight. Scion and Gaitar jolted forward from opposite sides of the lake, and suddenly the dark mists covered them again. Malithaia boasted a deep roar of laughter with his trickery.

"It won't be that easy." The monster's teeth were exposed as he grinned with delight at the army's growing fear and dispair. "The offer stands. Your pathetic little creatures against my children. You win, you get your other pitiful friends. If I win, I get to keep them..." Malithaia leaned down, his snout so close to Scion that he could feel the heat of his breath upon his fur, "and I get to keep you all."

A frown crossed Scion's face at this proposal. It

seemed like an easy out, his army outmatched him in number alone, but easy seemed highly unlikely from something so sinister. There must be a hidden motive, but Scion could not think of one. He looked across the lake to Gaitar, whom he could barely see through the mists, but he could make out an affirmative nod from his elder. Scion looked back up to Malithaia with his answer.

"We accept your challenge. We defeat your palawals and you let our gean go free."

The glowing red eyes narrowed, and a devious smile emerged through the shadows and exposed long, jagged black teeth.

"Very well."

Malithaia raised his head and roared out his call to beckon forth his children. The dark mists swirled around the lake, coming from the mountain crevices and shadows from under the wilted trees, and took forms around Scion's armies. Beasts in great number appeared on the ground before them, at least two to one, and the troops were frozen in place with fear. Terrifying faces with broad snouts, sharp teeth, and piercing little eyes that made the army feel like they were devouring their souls from afar. They held their body upright using their thick back legs that had a singular long talon, and short arms that had three fingers with long talons as well. Their long tails swayed from side to side as each of them stretched their back legs after a long slumber. The head and neck seemed similar to the Kaizankuri, but more fierce and smaller in stature. Malithaia's children approached the armies from all ground angles, unleashing harsh screeches into the air and resonating through the canyon.

The monstrosity grinned maliciously as he declared war. "You will now witness the might of Malithaia. Attack!"

The shadow children screeched in unison and darted forward as commanded. Blades slashed through the air, missing their mark as the demons dodged and jumped out of the way, and then attacked back. The clan swiped with their talons and tails, lunged with their massive heads to use their treed crowns as an advantage or bear down with their teeth, but they were much too slow to match the speed of their foes. The tribe was also unmatched in their speed to swipe blades in attack against these foul creatures.

Screams from the Dolgaian and Kaizankuri being bitten and torn to shreds made Scion's heart ache. Blades and talons were swinging through the air, but they were never trained to fight. Flesh and fur were flying off of his kin as they were bitten into, and he watched them die before his eyes. As Scion swung his blade at a shadow beast, fighting it off to save himself, he watched another shadow jump from the air and strike down one of his kin. The Dolgaian male fell quickly, and his eyes remained open as he lie there lifeless. Thick hide was being gashed as peppulas and leaves fell from the clans' brows in their fight. The army was ill prepared for a pack of adversaries such as these. A deafening ringing tone began pounding in Scion's ears. He was watching his brethren fall and being mauled as he continued to swipe his blade at the beasts coming his way. *Did I choose the wrong path? Did I bring them this far to simply fail?*

A low rumbling sound was coming from the mountain pass and vibrations gave sensation under hoof. As Scion fought off another attacker, he briefly turned his sights to see what was behind them, fearing it was more of Malitaia's children coming to lay waste to his army. As the pounding sound got closer, he saw Jantu's face leading the Natiko into the Eye at full speed. His tribe was carrying Cacicos on their backs as well to add to the number of reinforcements. Malithaia roared with anger at the surprise army coming to defend Ocaia, and the new army sprang into action. Cacicos leapt from their perches to grab the faces and tails of their attackers while the Natiko came in to bite at the legs. Relief began to run through Scion's body as he then pushed forward his own attack, swinging his blade to slay the attackers. A shadow beast ran passed Scion and he saw a Cacico riding on it, with its tail wrapped around the enemy's neck, and a Dolgaian swiped a blade to cut it down.

"Scion, get on my back!" Kalra called out as he ran and lowered his body to hoist up Scion.

Scion ran toward the Lord of the Sky, grabbing a spike on his back to brace himself for a quick flight. Rising into the air, Scion cut through a few beasts that attempted to take out his ride. One swipe of his blade and they disappeared in a black cloud of dust. They could not hold on with their short arms, and while their back legs were incredibly strong it was not enough to keep balance off the ground. Kalra suffered a few slashing cuts from the shadows during the crossfire, but quickly shot through the air once there was no more hindrance on his back. Scion suddenly realized they had the advantage with their winged friends and the new ground army below.

"Get off the ground! Fly! Fly!" Scion called out to his kinship below.

Gaitar heard his call and looked up in the sky to see Scion riding Kalra. He searched around for his closest flying options, finding the green and gold Zephra being attacked by two beasts. She screamed in agony as the marred her skin and tugged her wings. Gaitar ran forward at full speed in her direction, unleashing a deep throated roar while holding his blade in a striking pose. He leapt into the air, slashing one at her neck as he came down the dirt, then when he landed he jumped as high as he could to swipe at the one on her back. When she was free, he sat at the base of her neck while holding her back blades.

"Can you fly?"

Zephra nodded and began to flap her wings as she went bounding over the ground and took off into the air above.

Kalra and Scion circled the canyon before spotting an opportunity below. With Takenna's sword, he pointed to a mass of beasts below that were convening on their second army and Kalra immediately turned and dove in that direction. Scion held onto the grass-like blades upon Kalra's back as he leaned down to the side, and while the Kaizankuri cut through the air Scion slashed through four beasts in a matter of seconds before Kalra ascended once more.

The Dolgaian followed suit once they saw the advantage waiting in the sky, jumping on the backs of the clan with some carrying multiple members, becoming warriors on winged creatures. They were swooping down and diminishing the beasts one by one. Their foes could jump with their strong legs, but they could not fly. The Natiko and Cacico tribes kept them distracted or held down while the Dolgaian swooped in to take out the shadow minions.

Scion extinguished the last shadow child of Malithaia, flying through the thich air and hanging on for dear Takenna's life, and cheers broke out across the valley. Dolgaian were waving their blades above their heads and the Kaizankuri were roaring with glorious victory. Cacicos and Natiko were dancing on the ground below. Celebration was cut short when Malithaia unleashed a blood curdling scream, screeching and snarling at his children's defeat. Scion directed Kalra to land at the bank of the lake, in front of Malithaia. Then he dismounted and approached on hoof, holding his gifted sword tightly while speaking to the monstrosity before him.

"Malithaia. Your children are defeated. Give us our gean, as promised."

A twitching sneer rolled across the large, dark face. The black water dripping from his snout became thicker as he showed his teeth, and his red eyes glowed brighter with rage. The tension could be seen coursing through his body, shadows flowing rapidly across his form, and the lashing of his tail behind him. The sight made Scion grow uneasy about this exchange, but he held his composure.

"You cannot defeat me, and Takenna cannot defeat me from the void. I am reclaiming what is rightfully mine!" Malithaia was adamant, and on the last word his massive snout snapped his teeth together in front of Scion. He slapped his front claws on top of the lake in solid defiance.

Scion stood his ground, chest out and hooves hard set in the ground beneath him. He was not going to be intimidated, despite the stark difference in size. He glanced down at Takenna's sword in his paw, shining in crystal light and colors like his Goddess, then turned to look over his shoulder at Kalra. Surrounded by the second army behind him, Kalra nodded as if he knew exactly what Scion was planning. He smiled and turned his attention back at the monster over the lake.

"Perhaps you're right. The Goddess of Life may not be able to defeat you from within her confines. But here in Ocaia... we... can!"

The Fall of a Hero

Scion jumped backward, high into the air, and Kalra swooped his neck down to catch him mid-air before taking off into the sky. Malithaia watched and growled at them, turning his body to keep an eye on the pair as the army circled above him. The clan continued to fly overhead, ready to fight the fowl beast and take back Ocaia.

"You are fools to think you can defeat me!"

Malithaia arched his neck and lifted his head toward the sky, emanating a deafening scowl that caused the dark mist to swirl around him. Shadows from the mountains began to dart from side to side and closer to their master. His form, too, began to morph and become more fiery. The Eye of Takenna lake beneath him also changed from pitch black and began to glow in hues of red light under his large claws. The Natiko had started to run toward Malithaia, but the water had heated up the banks surrounding the water and they were unable to approach. Reluctantly, Jantu signaled his tribe to move back and watch the fight from a distance.

The clan had lost several of their own, and their riders also depleted in numbers from the first battle. The Kaizankuri struggled to maintain their balance in the air as the shadows and mist swirled around their master, but strong wings and mighty hearts fought the gale currents until the air finally stilled. Methodically, they teamed together to tackle the mighty beast.

Shadow and fire ruffled along Malithaia's back as he roared at his attackers in the sky. As he called out, balls of fire wrapped in shadow sprang from his body and shot through the air to attack the army overhead. Most of the clan were able to dodge the attacks, but a few were hit with repeated shots. Zephra and Gaitar stayed successfully in the air when he turned his attention to Taltaira and Caipri still bound by shadows against the mountain's edge. Gaitar motioned to Zephra, and they flew through the air at a rescue attempt while their adversary was temporarily distracted, but were knocked out of the sky by a stray shadow ball. As they plummeted to the ground, Zephra wrapped her wings around Gaitar as they descended to the ground below.

Scion and Kalra led attempts to attack Malithaia from several angles, searching for a weakness. Each attempt was useless against the rain of shadow fire, claw swipes or bites from the mighty snout made at them by the beast. The second army below was roaring and cooing as the Cacicos were throwing rocks to try and distract the monster.

"There is no weakness to exploit, Scion." Kalra turned his head slightly backward to speak to his rider.

Scion looked at his army, half in the air and half laying on the ground below while writhing in pain. He turned his sights to his sword, took a deep breath, and felt he knew the right path of attack.

"Come on, Kalra." He pulled the Lord of the Sky to the right while signaling the army to go left. Once they were in position, he then signaled the army to attack from their position. Scion clutched onto Kalra's trees as the force of wind shook the leaves, and he had trouble keeping his hoofing as they sped downward to the enemy. Adrenaline pulsed through Scion's veins as he watched the monster grow closer, and he felt his own end was nearing. Malithaia turned unexpectedly, long mouth gaped open, ready to eat his attacker and eyes focused on revenge for the inconvenience to his plans. Scion leapt off of Kalra's head toward his opponent, sword held tightly in his paws, as he plunged straight through Malithaia's shadow being and landed in the fiery-black lake below.

Agonizing wails erupted from the demon and shook the mountains. Malithaia's black body began to rupture in all directions as he cried out in defeat and a sharp wind circled the canyon. The Kaizankuri and their riders were thrown from the air, twisting them down and around into the mountain sides as they were unable to glide through the turbulent gales. The Natiko shielded their little riders from the harsh winds and falling rocks tumbling from the mountain sides. The demon continued to scream as his body diminished, and the gusts swirled closer around him until the dark cloud was completely dispersed.

The wind ceased, and the darkness subsided. Oreon light shined through the white clouds and the Eye of Takenna restored to a light, shimmering blue once more. The army was slow to get up with aches from their sudden journey to the ground in the aftermath of defeating their enemy. Mild sounds of celebration began to emerge amongst them as they embraced one another. Gaitar shook himself out of his muddled confusion and could see Caipri and Taltaira laying on the ground, no longer bound by the shadow bonds, and he sprinted toward them.

Kalra stood on the banks of the holy lake and looked around.

"Where is Scion?"

Celebration stopped and everyone converged on the lake, looking down into the water. They waited, but there was no sign of Scion. Dismay fell upon them, heads bowed and ears flattened behind their heads in solidarity to acknowledge their fallen hero.

◆ ◆ ◆

Scion could feel the air being expunged from his lungs. Deeper he fell into the water, unable to move his limbs. He could see the oreon light shining on the water above through his heavy eyes. He closed his eyes and accepted his fate as his task was complete and Caipri had been saved. Succumbing to the water filling his airways, he was struggling as the water entered and began to snuff out his life.

Darkness closed in around Scion as his final breath extinguished. Memories of his midawal and his sister were playing through his mind. He and Jiana were climbing a tree with friends when Scion accidentally kicked her off of a branch, launching her downward to

Ocaia and her ear was scarred while catching a branch on the way down. The first time he met Caipri, in the Kaian and by the Fountain of Takenna, her blue eyes twinkling in the oreon light as she introduced herself and he quickly fell in love. Midawal making her famous honey tarfe while he and Jiana were but small palawals. All of the fondest memories whipped through his mind before his end came to pass. Darkness entered Scion's mind and all thought ceased.

"Scion."

His eyes opened and he flailed as he gasped for breath. He was still floating in the water, but now encased in a safe haven that allowed him to breathe. He was mobile enough to move his body slightly to get upright with the top of the lake now above his head. Soft streams of color broke through the deep water and circled around him like the colors of the crystal void where he met his Goddess.

Takenna's form appeared before him in the colors amid the darkness, a mirrored reflection of herself from within her confines.

"Thank you, Scion. Malithaia is no more." Scion bowed his head while floating in the abyss of the lake. He looked up, and then back at the Goddess of Life. She giggled in return, which caused the water to glow is bright silver and blue tones throughout. "You can speak here. I have sheltered your body from the water entering."

She reached out her long, slender hand to him and appeared to touch his face, thought Scion did not feel her touch.

"I have a gift for you, in return of your valor."

Takenna gently waved her hand and the motion turned him around. Through the dark water, a glimmering light began to appear and came closer. A misty form at first, lit in light blue, began to take shape and in front of Scion was another Dolgaian male. They floated there in the water, staring at one another, and the other Dolgaian was smiling at Scion.

"Scion," he said as he clutched his paws to his chest, "my palawal."

"Padiwal?"

Sciotain nodded and Scion swam to embrace him. They hugged for a moment, again not feeling the full sensation of touch, but this was the first time in his life that he embraced the comfort of his padiwal. Scion filled with tears to finally meet Sciotain after all of the years of life having never known him.

"Scion, I am so sorry." Sciotain pulled away to look him in the eyes.

Scion shook his head and replied, "Padiwal, there is nothing for you to be sorry about. Takenna showed me your memories, and there was nothing more that you could have done. Midawal did the best she could with Jiana but I fear my sister is a lost cause."

They laughed together and then Scion noticed another blue glimmer approaching. This one morphed into Shawartia, who embraced her mate and then turned to Scion.

"My palawal," she gracefully reached for his cheek as she spoke, and Scion leaned into her motion. "I am proud of you. Takenna guides you."

"We must go now," Sciotain said while clutching Shawartia's paw, both of them looking at their palawal with pride.

"Good-bye, Padiwal. Midawal. Takenna guides you."

Smiles crossed their faces before they drifted back into soft, shimmering light and disappeared.

Scion paddled his way back around to face his Goddess.

"Thank you."

Takenna graciously smiled in return and came closer.

"I shall return you. Caipri was certainly right about you. You are one of my special children, my Chosen Child."

The water spiraled around and lifted Scion toward the light. He flailed while trying to stabilize his body through the assent, breaking through the glass-like water and into the canyon air. The wave carried him out of the lake and gently placed him on the bank in front of his friends.

Cheers erupted and members approached to slap him on the shoulder. Jantu, along with the Natiko and Cacico, ran up on the army to share in the celebrations. Dolgaian were apprehensive at first, but after a couple of moments they realized this was a victory for all of Ocaia and embraced the odd army that had come to assist them. Kalra looked down with a smile, grateful his rider returned safely. The clan roared in celebration while flapping their wings with excitement. All the while, Scion was peering through the crowd to find Caipri. He saw Gaitar, walking toward him slowly with his head bowed and holding his left arm, and Scion ran to meet him.

"Caipri? Is she safe?"

Gaitar looked up at Scion and smiled, then moved to the side to show Caipri and the others behind him.

"They are still weak, but they are alive. Thanks to you." Gaitar laid a paw on Scion's shoulder and then pushed him toward his palawal.

Caipri walked toward Scion, weariness noticeable on her brow, but a slight smile on her face. Scion ran and grabbed her in a hug, his paws holding her back and the nape of her neck.

"You got my message." Caipri spoke low but there was humor in her tone.

Scion released her from his grasp and laughed, holding her paws in his and touching his forehead to hers. The two of them sighed heavily in relief during the embrace. He then untied a piece of his blade sash and showed her the oreon circle.

"Be careful not to lose this again, Sesuna." He winked and handed the gift to her.

Caipri smiled and replied, "Please, call me Caipri."

Scion looked upon the escort, those of Prima Dair as well as other regions he was unfamiliar with and took it all in. Creatures he had never seen or read of before stood before him as they all relished in the glory of saving Ocaia. He saw Maichin toward the back and walked to him, extending a paw out and they shook.

"Maichin. Jiana will be glad to see that you are safe."

Maichin's smile turned to a screwed up face as he didn't understand the meaning, but Scion walked back to Gaitar and Caipri before he could inquire about the statement.

A tapping was felt on Scion's hoof, and he looked down to find Olicai staring up at him. Scion opened his arms, and the white bird jumped and nestled under his neck. Scion stroked Olicai's feathers for a moment before pulling him away to speak with him.

"I missed you too, bird."

The ground began to shake, and the Eye of Takenna began to swirl around to open a whirlpool in the middle. Rumbling sounds echoed between the mountains as specks of light erupted from the middle of the lake and dispersed around the mountains. Trees came back to life, grass grew lush in dark green on the ground, shimmering blue peppulas began to sprout across the mountain sides, and blue birds started flying in the sky above. Everyone stood in awe at the sudden change and blossoming of Takenna's Life around them.

When the lights stopped coming from the lake, the form of Takenna herself emerged from the gathering of the lanarai above the water. Her form perfectly reflected by the lights of the bugs creating her. The Goddess of Life commanded the air around her with her size and demeanor, but in a soft manner. Birds came to flutter around her and all tribal members of Ocaia knelt before her glowing silhouette.

"My children. Please, stand." Everyone did as they were told, and Takenna continued. "Scion, please step forward."

Scion placed Olicai in Caipri's arms, then turned around and approached Takenna as requested.

"My Chosen Child, do you solemnly swear to uphold my request and unify the tribes?"

"I do, my Goddess."

Takenna bowed her head, and Scion returned the gesture. She then turned her attention to the others.

"The Eye of Takenna is now safe, thanks to all of you. Remember this day. May you all share the victory for generations to come. This land has now been restored to its natural beauty. Chosen Palawals are no longer required to remain here in my honor. Any of those that wish to venture here shall be welcomed in my embrace, and those that choose to stay among their tribes may continue to do so. Your destiny is your own."

Takenna looked directly at Caipri with her last statement, and tears began to fill Caipri's eyes. Her life sentence of solitude was lifted by the Goddess herself, and she was free.

Takenna raised her arms to the sky and the Eye of Takenna swirled even faster beneath her. Then, in the blink of an eye, the lights creating her form dispersed with a sharp brush of wind that spread throughout the valley. She was gone and the lake became stilled. Minor celebrations and discussions took place among them, but Scion turned to Caipri, Taltaira and Gaitar.

"Well, I think it's time to rest before we make the long journey back to Prima Dair. I'm exhausted."

Caipri responded with soft eyes and gentle smile, reaching out to Scion's paw. "I cannot wait to go home."

Jantu approched with the Natiko and Cacico tribes.

Scion stood tall as the massive animal came and bowed before hime. Scion returned the gesture and they both smiled at one another.

"Jantu. How did you come to aide us in the attack?"

He huffed before he responded. "A swarm of lanarai came through the trees and requested assistance at the Eye of Takenna. Something about the Chosen being in danger. I thought they meant the Chosen Palawals, but now I see that it was you."

They bowed their heads again to say good-bye and Scion watched as the Southern neighbors set up a place to rest. Scion suddenly had a thought and his face began to frown. He looked up at Kalra.

"Lord of the Sky, we were so eager to venture here to save Caipri that I never asked you the same thing. How did you know that we needed assistance?"

Kalra grew a large grin as he responded, "A bird told me."

Tribal Reunions

It had been seven days since her brother left to save the Sesuna. Jiana could not focus on making tarfe and could barely bring herself to harvest honey from the baicher nests outside. In fact, she couldn't remember the last time she had something to eat. Her heart was pained and broken, faced to deal with the anxiety on her own. She mostly laid on her resting bunk, unable to sleep when she desired it and unable to stand when she knew she should be working. Scion was right, she needed a mate, or someone, in her life. The loss of her midawal, then the sudden departure of Maichin, followed by the unknown situation of Scion was too much for her to physically bear.

Voices began to become louder outside of her window as Dolgaian were gathering in the Kaian. Jiana lifted her head slightly, but she could not make out discernable words. She shook her hazy state and began to get off of her bunk, confused what the fuss could be all about. Unstably, she made her way through the dorsa and opened the front door to see females and palawals gathered around and looking to the sky while yelling and waving. Jiana looked up and saw Kaizankuri circling overhead. Suddenly she felt rejuvenated and hope leapt back into her soul.

Kalra descended into the Kaian and everyone moved back to allow space for him to stand. Scion, Caipri, and Olicai were perched on his back and jumped down to greet their tribe. Jiana rushed through the crowd and wrapped her arms around Scion's neck.

Her grasp was tight and Scion started to tap her arm so she would release him. They laughed and touched foreheads while holding paws.

Zephra then landed in the Kaian, Gaitar and Taltaira in tow. The other Kaizankuri landed outside of the Kaian perimeter and Dolgaian began rushing in to greet their loved ones after the hard fought victory.

There was cheering, as well as crying from some that had loved ones that did not return. Gaitar looked at Scion and then tilted his head toward the tribe, a signal that it was now his turn to address the Dolgaian as a leader. Scion looked at Caipri and Jiana, who smiled in return, and he moved forward to speak to his tribe.

"Dolgaian! Our Sesuna and our escort has been saved, but we lost some very valuable lives in our efforts. Do not despair, for their sacrifice gave Ocaia its freedom from pure evil. Takenna guides us all, and she has called upon me to unify the tribes of Ocaia. Prima Dair answers the call of the Goddess of Life."

In unison, the Dolgaian and Kaizankuri yelled, "Takenna guides us!"

Jiana looked at her brother, her heart grew full of relief as she as spoke. "What happened at the Eye of Takenna?"

Scion looked at her and replied, "I will tell you all about it after we rest. It's been a long journey."

❖ ❖ ❖

Large ears took in the sounds of birds whistling through the land. Large eyes closed, focused on other senses taking in the light without sight. Laying on their bellies, Scion and Caipri soaked up the oreon light on their backside in a trance with the happenings around them. He opened his eyes, large and the lightest shade of gold, looking into her eyes of icicle blue. They smiled at each other, then rolled over to their backs to stare at the sky above.

The ground gave sounds that someone was on the approach. Scion and Caipri sat up to see Jiana and Maichin coming and it appeared they had a tarp full of tarfe.

"May we join you for a meal?" Jiana said as she looked down at her brother in the grass, a large smile upon her face as her arm was intertwined with Maichin's.

"Sure, Jia. Come sit with us. What do you have in the tarp?"

"Honey Tarfe, of course." Maichin replied as the pair sat down.

"I have also tried my paw at making a new flavor of tarfe. This one is made with fruit from your brush as well as honey. Please tell me what you think."

Jiana gave the group the new tarfe recipe first and they took a bite. Everyone gasped with delight as drool filled their mouths.

"Jia! This is incredible! Your best recipe yet."

Caipri interjected her opinion, "Oh, yes definitely! I mean, Shawartia was a genius making tarfe with honey but this is just as divine. Maichin, I think you've found a keeper here."

Maichin and Jiana looked at each other, love written in their eyes as they took each other's paw.

"Scion," Maichin said, "I wanted to ask you, since Sciotain and Shawartia are no longer with us-"

"No." Scion blurted out a response while eating tarfe, not looking in their direction and focused on the food in his paw.

Jiana's eyes grew wide with outrage. "Scion! What in Takenna's-"

"-name is wrong with me?" Scion turned to look at Jiana and Maichin with a sly smile across his face.

Caipri shoved him and said while giggling, "Come on, now. Don't be so cruel."

They all laughed and Scion turned to Maichin. "I would be honored for you to take my sister off of my paws."

The four of them ate, talked, and laughed, then walked back to the Prima Dair Kaian as oreon was lowering toward the horizon. Jiana and Maichin parted ways back to their respective dorsas, while Scion and Caipri went to sit at the Fountain of Takenna. He took up her paw as they watched the water trickle from the stone Takenna's hand and down to the pool below.

"This fountain doesn't do her justice," said Caipri.

"No, it doesn't. It's hard to recreate someone so beautiful into a stone form. Speaking of, I have to begin unifying the tribes soon. I'm not entirely sure what to say, or what to do."

"You'll find a way, Scion."

"What if they don't listen?"

Caipri scooted toward Scion, leaned her forehead against his and clutched his paws within hers.
"Takenna guides you."

The End

Warning From Josima Mora

Caipri and Jiana rushed around the dorsa gathering peppulas and fur-fluffing for the big day. It was traditional for a midawal to assist with preparations, but Shawartia had joined with Takenna two cold cycles ago. Caipri was the closest to a sister Jiana could have, or could have asked for, during this time. Anxiety was seeping in and Jiana was finding it difficult to regulate her breathing as she paced around the table.

"Jiana, calm down." Caipri was fidgeting with peppulas and giggling at her friend. As Jiana was having a panic attack, Caipri was tying peppulas of blue and white into a wreath to sit on Jiana's brow.

"How can I calm down? This has to be the biggest day of my life, and what if we get there and Maichin doesn't show up? Or, what if we're standing there and his sense comes back to him and he says he made a mistake?"

"Jiana," Caipri grabbed Jiana's face in her paws and looked her straight in the eyes. "Maichin loves you and he will be there. Say it with me."

In unison they spoke, "Maichin loves me and he will be there." They both took a deep breath, and Caipri released Jiana's face.

Scion walked through the door to check on them, seeing as they were already late to meet before the big ceremony.

"Jia! Look at you, my tall and gorgeous sister!"

"Don't start with me, Scion. My nerves can't handle you patronizing me right now."

Caipri looked at Scion and rolled her eyes, a silent display of how she was coping with Jiana at this time.

"Jia, Jia, Jia. I am not patronizing you." He walked up to her and tucked a knuckle under her face to make her look in his bright, golden eyes. "You look wonderful and Maichin is lucky that you have decided to be his mate. Trust me." He rested his forehead on hers and then backed up.

With more resolve than before, Jiana straightened up and took a deep breath. She nodded at Caipri, who had finished her work on the peppula wreath and placed it over Jiana's ears to rest above her face. Scion took up the bunch of peppulas from the table and brought them over to his sister. She took them in her paws and took another deep breath.

"Alright. I'm ready... I think."

Caipri and Scion laughed as they headed out the door and into the Kaian where the entire Dolgaian tribe cheered for the mate to be. Jiana was blushing as Scion and Caipri led her through to the Fountain of Takenna, where Maichin was eagerly waiting.

Scion took his place next to Maichin, Caipri stood

beside Jiana, and Gaitar began to officiate the union ceremony.

"Dolgaian. We gather in the Kaian to witness the union of Maichin and Jiana. Before Takenna we stand in solidarity as-"

Gaitar's speech was cut short as a hard, bitter cold wind swept through the Kaian. Everyone tucked down as the air nipped the skin beneath their fur coats. Maichin covered Jiana, but Scion was unable to walk against the currents to Caipri. As the tribe struggled to stand against the gale, a Kaizankuri was being thrown through the air and landed in the Kaian.

As suddenly as the chill air appeared, it disappeared. Scion shook it off and checked on Caipri, then turned his attention to the Kaizankuri. It was Kalra, Lord of the Sky and leader of the clan. Caipri and Scion ran to him and checked for injuries before speaking with him.

"His trees. His beautiful pink trees are breaking." Caipri stated with a quiver in her voice, partly from the cold air but also with fear that their friend was in danger.

"Kalra," Scion said. "Kalra! Are you alright?"

Kalra opened his eye and looked at Scion. His large, yellow eye and oval black pupil were half-covered as his lids were unable to open fully.

"Josima Mora. The Taigolas... are... in trouble."

Caipri leaned forward. "What happened, Kalra."

"The cold grew colder. A shriek rang through the air as ice rained down from the sky. Something. Something attacked us during our mission. I was able to fly, barely, and escaped." Kalra coughed, his strength waned as he spoke.

Scion stood and began to give orders.

"Taltaira, please tend to Kalra. Gortainin, gather the clan and alert them that the Lord of the Sky has fallen and we need their wings to get to Josima Mora immediately."

Scion turned his attention to Jiana and Maichin. Jiana nodded as she was wrapped in Maichin's arms, signaling that it was alright for him to go. He mouthed I'm sorry and then looked at Caipri.

"Stay here with Jiana and make sure Kalra is well tended to during my absence."

"Oh, no. You are not going without me."

"Caipri, this is serious."

"And you're seriously not going without me. If the Taigolas are in trouble, you may need my help."

Zephra landed in the Kaian and nuzzled her mate. Sadness crept into her eyes as she helped to move Kalra out of the way for medicinal attention. Scion watched the Kaizankuri pair and a twinge hit his heart. If that were him and Caipri, she would be there for him. He looked up at Gaitar, who tossed the Blade of the Goddess and Scion snatched it from the air before turning his attention back to Caipri.

Caipri stared at Scion and said, "Let's ride."

ABOUT THE AUTHOR

K. J. Riley

K.J. Riley is a southern born woman that currently resides in Texas. She is married with three children and spends her free time with her family. They like to travel together and explore new destinations.

The Chosen Child: Tales of Ocaia is the first book written by this author and anticipation of Book II is already in production. Stay tuned for more Tales of Ocaia coming soon.